THE INTERPRETER

Also by Brian Aldiss
and available from New English Library:

THE DARK LIGHT YEARS
THE CANOPY OF TIME
SPACE TIME AND NATHANIEL
EARTHWORKS
THE AIRS OF EARTH
EQUATOR
COMIC INFERNO

The Interpreter

BRIAN ALDISS

NEW ENGLISH LIBRARY
TIMES MIRROR

*N E L Books are published by The New English Library Limited from Barnard's Inn,
Holborn, London E.C.1. Made and printed in Great Britain by Hazell Watson & Viney
Ltd, Aylesbury, Bucks*

4500 2713 9

A NOTE FROM THE AUTHOR

Science-fiction stories featuring galactic empires have always intrigued me, partly because I had the chance of seeing at first hand the uneasy relationship existing between "imperialists" and subject races in India and Indonesia. So there's a galactic empire in this book with Earthmen on the receiving end as subject race. The plot hinges on the notion that the further spread your empire is, the greater are the opportunities for graft therein.

So the villains of the piece are not so much the all-conquering *nuls*, as the size of the galaxy and the economics involved in its rule. At the same time, the fact that the four central characters each have good reason to mistrust the other three does complicate things.

I hope it doesn't complicate things too much. Van Vogtian complexities of plot and sub-plot are not for me. This book aims at being a simple study of four pretty hard types each trying to out-think the other.

—BRIAN W. ALDISS

Thought. Thought: that field of force still to be analysed. Thought: as inseparable from a higher being as gravity from a planet. It wraps around me, as my senses go about their endless job of turning all the external world into symbols. I can know no external thing without its being touched – perhaps in some unguessable way transmuted – by my thought.

The baseness I saw my own people, the nuls, perpetrating on that world Earth; was it real, or a misinterpretation in my mind?

Never the less, here and now, moneyless and far from home, I must prefer practical questions. My eyes must be on the main chance. Someone must be fleeced, so that I can get back. Thoughts are a gamble. Some days interesting ones turn up, some days dull ones. Maybe that's why I'm a gambler: I'm hoping to discover something more than chance behind chance.

Certainly my thoughts should be interesting now. Here I lie flat on the wide wall by the old harbour, gazing up at the universe. Because it is night, I can see the stars which belong to that empire in which I am a member of the master race.

My name is Wattol Forlie; I am a nul; I rest penniless but resourceful on a low wall on what is temporarily the night side of a planet that its misbegotten lopsided sons call Stomin. Is that not an interesting thought?

Not particularly. My feelings, my precious feelings, they are more important. Consider: I have no cause for optimism, yet I am optimistic. I am umpteen light years from Partussy, yet I am not homesick. I must appear to be in a drunken coma, yet my wits are as sharp as the beastly *vinn* I swigged at Farribidouchi's.

And there is another level of my thought, a danger level, coming into action. I have one eye cocked to the galaxy and one to my inner self. Yet at the same time I am aware of this thug sliding towards me from a side street. He skirts the worn wooden capstan, and the pile of offal and shells where the sea food stall stands during the day. He approaches like a villain.

He's a nul, I notice. Therefore arrogant, no doubt, as I am arrogant. He carries a knife with which to threaten me, the cheap quaint. How should he realize it is Wattol Forlie who sprawls here?

How could he imagine the thoughts in my head as brightly peppered as the stars up yonder, which will scatter when even-

7

tually he gets up enough pluck to stutter his "Put your hands up," or whatever melodramatic drivel he will utter?

Wattol Forlie let his thoughts pour out through his head, enjoying his own calm in the face of danger. For a nul, he had indeed some complexity of character. Yet even he, lying tipsy on a harbour wall on Stomin, had no inkling of that chain of events upon which the destiny of one world, and perhaps even of the galaxy, depended.

And had he known, in his present mood he might have done no more than wave an arm in dismissal.

Not that he was a fatalist. He believed in the importance of every action. He also believed that in a galaxy of four million civilized planets those actions would eventually cancel each other out.

As he was reflecting with delight on the involutions of his own character, a voice from three feet away said coldly, "Raise your hands and sit up, and keep quiet about it."

Wattol disliked such treatment, especially on an alien planet. He knew that the misshapen inhabitants of Stomin would happily melt him or any other nul down for the sake of his blubber content without thinking twice about it. Still making no attempt to move, he swivelled an eyestalk to observe his opponent.

Through the dark, he saw a tripedal figure much like his own.

"Does your being a nul entitle you to act like this?" he enquired lazily.

"Sit up, brother. I'll ask the questions."

Wattol spat.

"You're no ordinary thug, or you'd have had the sense to shut me up without all the dramatics. Come and tell me what you want like a civilized being."

The figure came nearer, angry now.

"I said sit up –"

As Wattol finally did so, he launched himself at the other, catching him just below the midriff. They fell heavily, and a long curved knife went spinning. Distant lamplight slanted on to their faces as they grappled together.

"Wait!" the attacker exclaimed. "You're the gambler, aren't you? Weren't you at Ferribidouchi's joint earlier, playing on the central tables?"

8

"Is this a time for conversation, you cheap quaint?"

"You're the gambler, aren't you? A thousand apologies, sir! I mistook you for an ordinary loafer."

They scrambled up, the attacker full of contrite and flattering phrases. His name, he declared, was Jicksa, and he humbly offered Wattol a drink to compensate for his deplorable conduct. The dark, he swore, had driven him to a foolish act.

"I like all this no better than your earlier behaviour," Wattol said. "The truth is, I want nothing to do with you. Be off and leave me alone in meditation, you squirt."

"I've an offer to make you. A good offer. Look, we nuls must stick together. That's the truth, isn't it? Stomin is a fearful place to be on. Because it happens to be a main conjunction of several important space routes, it swarms with all sorts of riffraff –"

"Like yourself!"

"Sir, I'm only temporarily down on my luck, just as you obviously are. Together we will re-establish our fortunes. I, you see, happen to be a gambler too."

"You might have said that in the first place, and saved yourself a lot of energy," Wattol said, beating dust and old fish scales from his clothing. "Let's go and get that drink. You can pay for it and tell me what your offer is."

They found a place called the Parakeet. It stank but was comfortable. None of the other life forms present were too revolting in appearance. Settling into a corner with their glasses, the two nuls were soon immersed in a discussion of various games of chance.

"I was fleeced when I was playing at Farribidouchi's. How comes it you have such an admiration for my playing?" Wattol asked.

Jicksa smiled.

"The game was rigged, of course, I was watching but I didn't say anything, or they would have cut my throat. It was a wonder you stayed in as long as you did. I figured we'd make a good pair when I saw the way you handled your cards."

"I certainly need the money. I've got a long way to get home; half the galaxy, no less."

"Where are you making for?"

"Partussy itself. I am a Partussian citizen, if that's any honour nowadays. They've treated me as shabbily as if I was a member of a junior race."

9

"I certainly don't owe the authorities any love either," Jicksa admitted. "What happened to you, if it's not a long story?"

"Until a few months ago, I was Third Secretary of a Commission on a planet full of bipeds. A nice comfortable job, but I couldn't bear the way the Commissioner, a fellow called Par-Chavorlem, was treating the locals. He was a hateful swine. So I up and complained, and he threw me out on my ear. Didn't even give me the fare to get home with – that's standard Foreign Department procedure, by the way.

"Well, I'd saved enough cash to buy a passage on a ship to Hoppaz II, and from there to Castacorze, which is a sector HQ planet. Castacorze is a foul dump, I tell you! Like most HQ planets, it's rotten with graft, but the ordinary citizen can't swing a thing. I was stuck there for a year until I had earned enough money for a passage here. I even did manual labour to earn it."

Jicksa tut-tutted in sympathy.

"Yes, but at least I did two useful things on Castacorze. I resolved that after the way I'd been treated the world owed me a living; from now on I'm going to rely on my luck and my wits to get me home to Partussy."

"At the rate you're going, friend, it'll take you twenty years. Stay here with me and fleece the tourists."

Wattol decided he did not much like Jicksa. The fellow seemed incapable of distinguishing between an ordinary crook and a man with extraordinary ambitions. Still, he would serve his purpose in the long game of leap frog that carried Wattol from planet to planet towards home.

Draining his glass, Jicksa signalled for another measure.

"What was this other useful thing you said you did on Castacorze?" he inquired.

Wattol grinned a sour grin.

"You've probably never heard of Synvoret? He's a big noise on the Supreme Council on Partussy. He always had a reputation in the Foreign Department for being one of the few incorruptible nuls left! So I got together a bundle of evidence against this Commissioner Par-Chavorlem and sent it off to Synvoret from Castacorze."

"What good will that do you?" Jicksa asked.

"Some satisfactions can't be bought for money, brother Jicksa. Nothing would give me greater pleasure than seeing this

10

louse Par-Chavorlem kicked out, and this planet he lords over getting a square deal. And Synvoret's the nul to do it."

Jicksa sniffed. He had met sacked civil servants with crazy grievances before.

"What did you say the name of this planet was where you worked under Par-whosit?" he asked, bored.

"Oh, a backward little dump called Earth. I don't suppose you've heard of it?"

Sipping his new drink, Jicksa agreed he had never heard of it.

I

The chair was very much in contrast to the coat that had been flung over it. Like the room in which it stood, the chair was large, over-ornate, and fearfully new.

The coat was simple in cut, worn, and old-fashioned. Made by a good Partussian tailor, it had the usual three bat-winged sleeves with apertures below the arms, and a high collar reaching almost to the eye-stalks such as was now worn only by members of the old school of diplomats. The edge of the collar was as frayed as the three wide cuffs.

This was the coat of Signatory Arch-Hiscount Armajo Synvoret. Ten seconds after he had dropped it over his ornate chair, the cupboard extended a hook and drew the worn garment into its embrace. Tidiness is a virtue for underlings and machines.

Ignoring this, Synvoret continued to pace round his new room. His life had been austere, dedicated to the furtherance of Partussian justice on other worlds. This chamber, at once frivolous and ostentatious, seemed to him to embody principals he had often fought against. He resented being moved from his old quarters into it, for all its boasted advantages.

Synvoret opened the first document on his desk. Inside its foil cover was another cover, a dozen gaudy stamps on it indicating its hopscotch passage from one port to another across the galaxy to its present destination. Its earliest stamp, marked CASTACORZE, SECTOR VERMILION bore a date almost two years old. With increased interest, Synvoret slit it open.

The envelope contained a number of flimsy documents and a covering letter which Synvoret read first:

"To Supreme Council Signatory Arch-Hiscount Armajo Synvoret, G.L.L., I.L.U.S., L.C.U.S.S., P.F., R.O.R. (Omi), Fr.G.R.T(P), Colony Worlds Council, Partussy.

"Sequestered and Honoured Signatory Sir: Since my name will hardly have penetrated through the hierarchies and light years which divide us, permit me to introduce myself. I am Wattol Forlie, one-time Third Secretary to High Hiscount Chaverlem Par-Chavorlem, Galactic Commissioner to the planet Earth. To save your Signatoryship the annoyance of referring to files, let me add that Earth is a Class 5c World in System 5417 of Galactic Administration Sector Vermilion.

"Good. I, Honoured Sir, have just been given the boot.

"I have not liked one single thing I have seen of the administration of this wretched planet Earth by our people. When I had the temerity to draft a minute to this effect to Commissioner Par-Chavorlem, I was brought before him and most unjustly given the push.

"You as a veteran of ministerial life will probably know the terms of the standard galactic-colonial contract for Grade Four rankers in the Colonial Service like me; by 'infringing' it, I have to find my own way home. With ten thousand light years to Partussy, I doubt if I shall see home again before I'm an old nul. An effective way of keeping anyone quiet, eh!

"However, Honoured Sir, my main gripe is not for myself but for the subject race of Earth, termed 'terrestials'. When and if you get to know them, these terrestials are pretty good creatures, sharing many of a nul's better characteristics. The fact that they are biped has told against them historically – as it seems to have done against biped races everywhere.

"My case is that these bipeds are being systematically exploited and ruined by our Earth Commissioner. Par-Chavorlem is greatly overstepping his lawful powers, as I hope the enclosed documents will prove to you. If his rule continues, all Earth culture will be obliterated in another generation.

"Par-Chavorlem should be stopped. A just nul should be put in his place, if just nuls can still be found. Our mighty, glorious empire stinks to heaven! It is rotten, decadent, through and through. If this dossier ever reaches you, I dare say you will do nothing about it.

"Why do I write to you in particular, Honoured Sir?

Obviously I had to write to one of the signatories of the Colony Council; they are the boys with the power to do things. I chose you because I learned that in your youth you held, among other posts, the position of Deputy Commissioner to Starjj, another planet in this sector, Vermilion, where your rule was a pattern for enlightened justice. You still have the reputation, I believe, for being honest and perceptive.

"If this is so, I beg you to do something for the terrestials, and post Par-Chavorlem somewhere where he can do no further harm. Or most probably you are too busy to trouble with this whole matter. This is the age of the Busy Nul!

"Your ex-servant in despair, I am, Honoured Signatory Sir, Wattol 'Big Head' Forlie."

The comb on Signatory Synvoret's leathery old head rippled in anger, an anger by no means directed entirely against Wattol Forlie. The Colonial Office, under a succession of inept Ministers, had in his view grown increasingly incompetent to manage its own affairs. As the years descended on his shoulders Synvoret grew increasingly sure that things were nowhere what they had been in his younger days. Forlie's letter seemed to confirm this.

He went over to the ornate chair, sat on it, and spread Forlie's dossier on the desk. Its contents were the sort of documents he had expected to find:

Copies of directions signed by Par-Chavorlem for internal circulation in the Commission, imposing racial restrictions.

Copies of an order to the military authorizing them to shoot on sight any terrestial found within half a mile of any main road.

Copies of instructions to terrestial authorities, inviting them to hand over art treasures to the Partussian authorities for "permanent safe keeping" against worthless guarantees.

Reports from Sub-Commission stations on Earth, giving details of forced terrestial labour gangs employed there.

And copies of several arrangements with civilian contractors, mining firms, managers of spacelines, and military governors – "one of the latter a Star General on Castacorze" – all showing items and expenditures well above anything prescribed for a 5c Commission.

It did, on the face of it, look like a major case of graft. The documents, most of which were photostats, built a sketch of systematic enslavement and robbery of the local population.

13

The Signatory had in his time inspected such documents before. The Partussian empire was far-flung; plenty of room existed in it for abuses. Corruption did flourish, however determinedly it was stamped on.

At the same time, and perhaps as frequently, disgruntled employees tried to ruin the bosses they imagined had ruined them.

Synvoret preserved an open mind. His brain was as cold as an old trout's. Rising, he walked over to the window, depaqued it, and gazed out at the forest of pinnacles which formed part of the biggest city in the galaxy. By craning his eye-stalks, he could just see the sky. Up there was Partussy's real estate; four million worlds of it. It was a sobering thought that no nul, no committee, no computer could know a billionth part of what went on there.

Without bothering to turn around, he rang the radio bell on his wrist. The young secretary appeared almost at once, smiling, flattening his comb. Perhaps Forlie was just another such upstart as this.

"What is my first item on today's programme?" Synvoret asked.

The secretary told him.

"Cancel it, please. I want you instead to check through to Central Records and get me all available data on Planet Earth of System 5417 GAS Vermilion, and on High Hiscount Chaverlem Par-Chavorlem, commissioner of that planet. And get me an appointment for tomorrow with the Supreme Councillor."

The Supreme Councillor's Ordinary Audience Room was tucked away in the centre of the same vast new block as was Synvoret's office. When Synvoret presented himself there, he felt relief to find the Councillor, an old nul called Graylix, alone with a robot recorder.

"Come in, Armajo Synvoret," he said welcomingly, rising to his three feet. "It is too long since we met informally."

"I warn you that I have a formal request to make of you, Supremo," Synvoret said, briefly interlocking an eye-stalk with his superior. "When my office made this appointment, I believe they sent you copies of certain documents?"

Graylix indicated a pile of blue flimsies on the table.

"You refer to the Forlie dossier? I have it here. Take a seat and discuss it if you so wish. It seems a matter more for

14

Psycho-Watch's Misdemeanor Branch than for us, don't you think?"

"No, Supremo, I don't. I came here to ask you to permit me to go to Earth."

The Supremo had sat down. Now he abruptly rose again.

"You wish to go to Earth? Why? To investigate the state of affairs there as reported by this sacked Third Secretary? You know as well as I do this evidence is probably false. How often have we not heard just such trumped-up charges from subordinates dismissed for some gross inefficiencies?"

Unmoved, Synvoret nodded.

"Perfectly true. All Forlie has sent us is documentary evidence, and modern forgery methods being what they are, we no longer trust documentary evidence. Worse, these only purport to be photostat copies. For all that, I feel challenged, and must request permission to travel to Earth to investigate affairs there."

"That can of course be done. In fact, it is easy. You would simply be given instructions to take a small Official Investigation Team to Earth."

"Then you will grant me facilities?"

The Supremo's comb made a noncommittal gesture.

"Officially, I suppose I can't refuse you. Reports of corruption must be confirmed or denied. Privately, however, I would like to remind you of a few facts. You are one of our most valued signatories. In your youth you saw active service in unpleasant fringe sectors like Vermilion. You have personal experience of a dozen Commissions. You're a tough old man, Armajo Synvoret –"

Signory Synvoret broke in with an embarrassed laugh, but his superior continued.

"– but you are old, and you must realize you are old, even as I am. Now you propose to visit some snivelling little mote of a planet two years warp-travel away. Four years you will be gone, four years at least, merely to gratify the whim of a moment. If you want a holiday, then by all means take a decent leave –"

"I want to go to Earth," the Signatory said, his comb stirring.

He took a turn about the long room, tugging at his arm flaps.

"We may be growing old nuls, Supremo, but at least we're the real thing. The honour of the Empire rests with us. You

15

know how these reports of corruption come in from time to time. It's about time someone responsible investigated them in person, instead of delegating authority to some Band of Hope Investigatory Mission which gets bribed on the spot and comes back reporting all's well. I cannot be bribed. I'm too pig-headed – and too rich. Let me go! If as you say it's the whim of a moment, then indulge me."

He stopped, aware that he had been speaking more harshly than he had intended. The remark about his being old had sunk in. The Supremo was smiling gently. That too irritated Synvoret. He hated being appeased.

"What are you thinking?" he asked.

The Supremo did not answer the question directly.

"When I received this Forlie dossier, I naturally checked with Central on this man. He is very young: fifty-six. He left Partussy for Earth with four thousand *byaksis* gambling debts."

"I also checked Central. Gambling debts make no nul a liar, Supremo."

The Supremo bowed his head.

"Yet Par-Chavorlem's record is clean enough."

"He is far enough away for any dirt not to be noticeable at this distance," Synvoret said dryly.

"So. Obviously, you are determined to go, Armajo. Well, you have all my admiration, though little of my envy. This oxygen-enfolded ball, Earth, sounds less than attractive. Get your secretary to attend Sessions tomorrow, and I'll submit you a draft list of Team applicants."

"I will keep the numbers to a minimum," Synvoret promised, rising. He would have a lot to attend to before leaving Partussy.

"And remember, Armajo Synvoret, that Commissioner Par-Chavorlem must be officially notified of your intended inspection."

"I would prefer to drop in on him unexpectedly!"

"Naturally, but protocol demands prior notification."

"So much the worse for protocol, Supremo."

When Synvoret was at the door, Graylix stopped him.

"Tell me, what really makes you suddenly so keen to venture on this quixotic errand to the other side of the galaxy? What, after all, is the future of one little planet out of four million to you?"

16

Synvoret raised his three arms in the nul equivalent of a wry smile.

"As you took care to point out, Supremo, I grow old. Perhaps justice has become a hobby with me."

He left. Back in his own quarters, he immediately drafted a signal:

"To Colony Worlds Commissioner High Hiscount Chaverlem Par-Chavorlem, I.L.U.S., L.G.V.S., M.G.C.C., R.O.R. (Smi), Earth, System 5417, GAS Vermilion.

"Commissioner Sir, You are hereby notified to hold yourself and your detail in readiness for my official and free-roving inspection of the planet Earth under your jurisdiction. I expect no special preparations for my visit. I do not give press interviews or attend cocktail parties or receptions other than requisite established minimum. No special demonstrations or appropriations need be made in my honour. All I shall require are facilities for unescorted travel and interpreter speaking Earthian language. Exact date of arrival follows. Synvoret."

II

Partussian jurisdiction over its mighty empire was strict but impartial. The nuls governed their subordinate worlds by slide-rule rather than emotion. Earth to them – at least to those far away on the Queen World of Partussy – was simply a 5c globe. This was an economic classification, the "5" standing for natural products, the "c" indicating an oxygen-nitrogen world.

The natural products were many, but in particular it was timber, tended and harvested by Earth men, that Earth exported.

Earth, in this its two thousandth year of Partussian domination, was covered with woods and forests, for the most part as neatly organized as factories. Some areas were not worth mass-production methods of afforestation, some had been given over to the rearing of *afrizzian* cattle. Here and there stood the old independent Earth cities and villages, some still partially occupied, some falling to ruins in forest clearings.

Everywhere ran the roads, good Partussian roads of vacuumized velcan, protected for every mile of their length by force fields. Before all else the Partussians were transporters, circulators. The road was virtually their symbol. Because they had been the first species to establish regular space routes, theirs was the biggest interplanetary empire.

One of these mighty roads ran across Eurore Division, across the fertile Channel Valley, to Greatbrit Division, where it swept into the ramparts of Commission City, chief nul centre on the planet.

Here, ensconced in his own official rooms in the palace, Commissioner High Hiscount Par-Chavorlem was reading a blue flimsy just delivered to him. He scanned it through twice before handing it to his companion, Arm Marshall Terekomy.

"This Synvoret sounds quite a bastard," he remarked.

"We've handled bastards berfore," Terekomy said.

"Yes, and we can handle Synvoret and his team. Big brass back home invariably turns into small fry when it reaches the fringes. Anyhow, it's splendid the way Colonial Service etiquette demands the early announcement of visitors. It gives us time to prepare. . . ."

He glanced at the date stamp on the letter.

"The fast warp-ships won't get Synvoret here much before two years objective time are up. So we've got that long to ensure that he sees only what we want him to see."

"Fine. We'll show him Earth's the best run planet in the sector," Terekomy said, sarcastically. "What worries me is why he's coming at all."

"Perhaps he's heard a rumour."

"Such as?"

"Such as the fact that the armed forces under you exceed by a factor of three the stipulated strength.

"Or that you personally pocket two *byaksis* for every spaceship that lands here.

"Or that you personally pocket two *byaksis* for every tree we export.

"Or that –"

"All right, Terekomy, we know where we stand. The point is that Partussy is no longer minding its own business. We have to be on our toes to frustrate their interference. Synvoret must see just what we want him to see and no more. Ring for a survey ship, will you? I think we'll start work right now by making a reconnaissance of the region. It must be all of three local years since I left Commission City."

The ship had arrived by the time they gained the top of the

building. It bore the two Partussians up through the enclosing force fields above the Commission, into the unbreathable atmosphere of Earth.

The Partussy Commission covered nine square miles of territory. Radiating from it along three points of the Partussian compass were the wide roads enclosed with force fields. Since the average nul weighed about a ton, land was generally preferred to air transport.

When an exploring scout of the mighty and ever-expanding Partussy Galactic Empire had first discovered Earth, some two thousand years ago, the inhibitants of that insignificant planet had been delighted to enter the Empire as fledgling members. The standard Protegé Charter had been signed.

At once, the advantages of Partussy's colossal material and technological superiority had been felt. Fabulous aid programmes sprang up all over the planet. Vast loans were floated. Development schemes were launched daily. Thousands of farsighted tripeds poured into Earth via the hastily-built spaceports, bringing with them their ideas, their money and their families.

Earth hummed with activity.

"A new renaissance!" the optimists exclaimed, echoing Partussy propaganda.

The wonderful new roads, slashing over terrestial highways, were soon constructed. Enclosed in their force fields, weatherproof and air-conditioned, they were the wonder of all Earth, even when it was discovered that they were intended for Partussian traffic only.

As, one by one, and each according to schedule, the astounding new schemes came to fruition, it dawned upon terrestials that the Partussy-Earth Co-Prosperity Sphere was just a mockery, its advantages operating only in one direction. Men were not even allowed to leave their own system, except to visit a few specified frontier worlds as semi-slave labour.

When this realization came, it was already too late to do anything effective. Perhaps it had always been too late. Partussy had over two million years of history behind it, and four million planets under its sway. Its diplomatic corps was made up of astute men who did not budge an inch under the growing chorus of terrestial protest. They behaved with that cruelly unwavering patience displayed by the keepers of mentally deficient children. If they were unfair it was legally so. Commis-

19

sioner after Commissioner coped gently with the obstreperous bipeds, striving to maintain goodwill where little cause for it existed.

Par-Chavorlem had changed all that. Taking up the post of Commission to Earth twenty-three years ago, he had instituted a system of graft that made him one of the most powerful, most hated, nuls in GAS Vermilion, a region embracing six thousand stars.

As he rode with his Arm Marshall now, high above the plains of Earth, he could see occasional burned fields of grain and shattered forests marring the orderly landscape. These were the results of guerilla activity which had broken out in protest against his extortions. All over the globe, terrestials were up in arms, fighting to destroy what would otherwise fall to the alien.

"The guerillas are not effective enough," Par-Chavorlem remarked, gazing down. "Before this inquisitive signatory arrives, we must damage our own plantations and burn arable land about the Commission. He should get the impression that these rabble biped bands are a serious revolt. We must portray ourselves as people beleaguered."

Marshall Terekomy agreed enthusiastically. "That would excuse the strength of our army here," he said. In his great cold tri-valve heart glowed respect for the Commissioner's lithe imagination. It spurred him to use his own.

"You know, we might even stage a little battle for our visitor," he said. "Let me think along those lines."

Below them slid a timber centre. A line of heavy transporters moved away from it towards the nearest space port. Par-Chavorlem's extortion methods were beautifully simple. Using as pretext the theory that a crowd of men might turn into a revolutionary mob, he had issued an edict twenty years ago limiting the number of men who might be employed by any one terrestial boss. This sent a flock of cheap labour into the hands of nul bosses. The money so saved, netted by an Employee Tax, found its way to the Commissioner's personal pocket.

"Let us get back," Par-Chavorlem snarled. His moods could alter suddenly, his customary urbanity falling away into anger. He was displeased that this change had come to disturb his life. The plane dipped round, heading for the City. Terekomy waited tactfully before speaking again.

"We have spread ourselves in recent years, Chaverlem," he

said. "We have been comfortable, despite the foulness of this planet. Even Commission City itself is twice as large as statutory requirements stipulate for a 5c world. We can never justify that."

"Yes. You are correct. The base personnel of Partussy expect us to live like pigs. The present city will have to be abandoned entirely and camouflaged against the prying eye of any signatory. We must build and occupy a temporary Commission of statutory size on a new site. We can then go back to normal when our Peeping Tom has gone."

Terekomy remained gazing thoughtfully at the hateful landscape drifting below. In his heart, however, blossomed once more the great admiration he felt for Commissioner Par-Chavorlem. Silently he thanked the Trinity that his lot had been cast here to serve beside this born leader of men, rather than in the decadent heart of the Empire.

Aloud, he said without emotion, "When we return, we will send for one of the terrestial representatives – your interpreter Towler would do – and get him to suggest a suitable site for the new building."

Chief Interpreter Gary Towler was shopping. In the afternoons when he was not required to work or wait at Par-Chavorlem's palace, he liked to do his own shopping, little as this might seem pleasurable in the circumstances.

The native quarter of Commission City was, of course, enclosed under the one big force dome, so that its lanes were full of the same noxious mixture of hydrogen sulphide and other gases as the rest of the Partussy enclosuré. The native quarter shops and flats had their own oxygen-nitrogen atmosphere, and were entered by airlocks. To go shopping required an air suit.

"I would like a pound and a half of that best shoulder bone cut, if you please," Towler said, pointing to a joint of *afrizzian* on the butcher's counter. *Afrizzians* were quick-breeding mammals imported from another planet in the sector. Large herds of them were at present being established on Earth.

The butcher grunted, serving Towler without speaking. Terrestials who actually came into contact with Partussians every day were despised even by terrestials who earned their living in the Commission by other means. They in turn were despised by the semi-voluntary labour gangs who were driven out of the Commission every night, who in turn were despised by the majority of terrestials who would and sometimes did starve

21

rather than deal with the aliens. A sort of scale of distrust divided the whole community.

Taking his grudgingly wrapped meat, Gary Towler clamped up the facepiece of his air suit and left the shop. The streets of the native quarter were almost deserted. They held no beauty; nor were they interestingly ugly. They had been designed by a nul architect on Castacorze, Sector HQ planet, who had seen bipeds only on sense-screens. His vision had materialized into a series of dog kennels. Yet Towler went his way rejoicing. Elizabeth should be waiting at his apartment.

The block of apartments in which Towler lived was small, three stories high only, entered or left by airlocks.

When he was through the double doors, he unclamped his face plate and hurried along the corridor, sorry that he could not comb his hair inside an air helmet. He opened the door of his three-room apartment. She was there.

The glimpse globe hung in the centre of the ceiling. Elizabeth stood directly beneath it. That was the only place in the flat from which her expression could not be spied upon. Towler's eyes lit at the sight of her, though he knew that his act of opening the door would click over a warning relay far away, so that now a nul – or even a man – would be bending over a screen, watching him come in, seeing what he carried, hearing what he said.

"It's good to see you, Elizabeth," he exclaimed, trying to thrust off self-consciousness, to forget the spy overhead.

"I shouldn't be here," she said. It was not a promising opening. She was twenty-four, slender, far too slender, her face spear-bright with its length, its keen blue eyes. She was not beautiful, but about all her features was a definition that gave her a quality more vivid than beauty.

"We can talk," he said gently. Living here alone, isolated, he had almost forgotten what it was to be gentle. Taking her hand, he led her to the small table.

Her every movement showed uncertainty. Only ten days ago she had been free, living far from the City, hardly seeing a nul from one month's end to the next. Her father was an *afrizzia*n canner with a small business. Then a fraud in his tax returns was detected. For five years he had been paying Partussy less than – under Par-Chavorlem's regime – was legally its due. His cannery was appropriated, his only daughter, Elizabeth, taken to work in the offices of the Commission.

There, scared and homesick, she had come under Towler's jurisdiction. Pity, and perhaps something more, compelled him to offer her what help he could.

"If we talk, can *they* not hear us?" she asked.

"Every word uttered goes to a monitoring post in Police HQ," he said, "where it is recorded. But of course they do not expect us to love them. Since they already have the power of life and death over us, a few words on tape hardly make much difference, only be guarded."

She flinched from the resignation in his words. He too belonged to a world quite foreign to her. They could touch each other, but as yet there was no real contact.

"Well then," she said, "how long must I expect to be kept here?"

It was his turn to flinch. He had worked here for ten years, ever since he was twenty, trapped on a charge even slighter than the one that had caught Elizabeth Fallodon. In all that time, he had never been out of Commission City. The nuls issued one-way tickets only to their biped attendants.

Instead of answering her directly, he said, "You will find it is not so bad here. A lot of very pleasant men and women work for the Partussians. And most of the Partussians, once you become used to their frightful exteriors, are inoffensive. It's fortunate you were drafted to Interpretation Branch. We are really quite a community on our own."

"I like Peter Lardening," she said.

"He is a promising young man, Lardening." As he spoke, aware of his own patronizing tone, Towler felt his cheeks redden. Lardening was indeed the best of the younger interpreters. Also, he would be about Elizabeth's age. It was too early to feel jealous, Towler told himself. Elizabeth was a stranger. For various reasons it was best she should remain a stranger.

"He seems very kind," Elizabeth said.

"He is very kind."

"And understanding."

"He is very understanding." Suddenly, he had lost the ability to make conversation. He wished to say that he was the Chief Interpreter; that he could help her the most.

It was almost with relief that he heard the communicator chirp, though at any other time it might have alarmed him. He smiled painfully as he turned from her.

"Hello," he said, going over to it. As his personal disc came within its search beam, so the screen lit. He recognized his caller as a minor clerk at the palace, a man, his face long familiar to Towler, though they exchanged nothing more intimate than a meaningless "good morning."

"Will you hurry on over to the palace, Gary Towler. Urgent call out for you."

"I have one afternoon off a month," Towler said. "This is it. Won't this urgent call keep fresh until tomorrow?"

"Commissioner himself's asking for you. Better hurry on over."

"All right. I'll be there. Don't panic!"

III

Sixteen and a half minutes later, Chief Interpreter Gary Towler was bowing to Commissioner High Hiscount Par-Chavorlem. After all these years of service in the City, Towler still felt a shudder of fear at the sight of a Partussian. Par-Chavorlem stood ten feet high. He was immensely solid. His great bulk was almost cylindrical, except for his arms and legs. A nul was like a canister to which two three-armed starfish were joined, one at the base, forming legs, one midway up, forming arms.

Like the rest of his kind, Par-Chevorlem was almost feature-less. At the end of each road arm were two flexible, opposed fingers, with retractable claws usually concealed. Near the top of his cylindrical body were three regularly spaced eye-stalks, while on top of his "head" was the usual fleshy comb. All his other features were concealed under the wide flaps of his arms; his mouth, his olfactory nerves, his aural cavities, his reproductive organs. A nul was a secret creature whose exterior betrayed very little.

Only the often highly expressive comb on the head relieved an impression of functional brutality.

"Interpreter Towler," Par-Chavorlem said, speaking without preamble in his own tongue. "Our way of life here will be altered from now on. Trouble brews, my little biped friend. Here is what you must do. . . ."

Some miles away, Arm Marshall Terekomy was peering at

24

a distant tower that looked to him as grim and forbidding as the Commissioner looked to Towler.

"And you say the terrestial rebel leader is in the tower?" Terekomy asked casually.

"His lookouts are, sir, and he is most certainly camped beneath it. That was why I radioed asking you to come here as soon as possible.'

The speaker was a Ballistics-Beadle Ibowitter, a nul new to Earth, commanding a team which manned the latest experimental field weapon, the stereosonus.

Terekomy was strangely calm.

"I see you were efficient, Ballistics-Beadle," he said.

"You'll find I do my very best, sir. I was posted here from Starjj, another biped world, sir, and there my reputation for efficiency was also high."

Still calm, Terekomy said, "I have seen your career sheet."

Slightly flustered by his superior's lack of enthusiasm, Ibowitter continued.

"And so I radioed you, sir, thinking you'd like to be in at the kill. This terrestial leader Rivars has been causing trouble for so long . . . I naturally thought that you. . . ."

His voice trailed off as he saw the colour of Terekomy's comb.

"If I've said anything, sir. . . ."

"Your career sheet," Terekomy remarked almost conversationally, "says that you were deported from Starjj because you murdered some two thousand bipeds in an experiment with this new weapon. On Starjj, from what I hear, the bipeds are treated a deal more leniently than they are here. There the rulers are enlightened. Here, thank Trinity, we aren't!

"Nevertheless, if you start knocking off terrestials with that infernal stereosonic weapon, I swear I will not merely deport you, I'll tear you in strips of blubber a millimetre thick."

"But, Arm Marshall, sir, this Rivars –"

"Rivars gives us a little opposition. Without him we have no excuse for restrictive measures. He costs us a lot every year, so we curtail his activities as far as possible. He's clever, I give you that, and if he had an offensive weapon like this new gadget of yours, it would be a very different story. But as it is, to wipe out his forces would be sheer folly, especially at present."

Peering through his air helmet, Terekomy surveyed the

broken terrain, the grey tower built of stone at a period long before the Empire had discovered Earth, and behind it the senseless, endless arrays of green foliage that flourished on this oxygen world. He sometimes had a cold fondness for this world. It was here he could be of service to Par-Chavorlem. He felt no anger for Ibowitter, only pleasure that he had stopped an unfortunate accident.

Ibowitter was apologizing.

"It's a pity we can't wipe out bipeds altogether," he said.

"Keep a thought like that to yourself. You know they're worth money. Millions of *byaksis* are invested in a little planet like this. How would the refineries, the factories, the mills, the farms, all the rest of it, work without biped labour? It would cost five times as much doing the job with robot labour."

"I have been briefed on the economic situation."

"Keep it in mind then."

Time to get back to the City and Par-Chavorlem, Terekomy thought. Here he was not at ease. From Ibowitter's hideout, little was to be seen but that old tower and the silent greenery perpetually breathing in its toxic carbon dioxide. In that greenery hid bipeds, terrestials. They could in theory be killed so easily. Yet always there was a reason – political, economic, personal, tactical – for not killing them. Perhaps they would at last survive to emerge from the greenery and take over again a world the nul had left. It was possible, for the bipeds admitted no compromise, whereas the Empire was founded on it.

Such thoughts made Terekomy gloomy.

"I did not mean to snap your head off, Ibowitter," he said. "I know you were doing what you thought was your duty, but your orders were only to contain Rivars. The truth is, we cannot do without a single fighting biped against us. In two years' time, we're going to need them to show a certain visitor how vicious they are."

"Sir?"

"Never mind. I'm talking to myself. Carry on, Ibowitter."

"Wait, Arm Marshall. You mean a time might come when you want to stage a fight or something with more bipeds?"

Terekomy continued to walk towards his car, which pointed sharply towards the city. He slowed his pace, otherwise revealing no interest.

"And what if so?" he asked.

26

Ibowitter became confidential, seeing he had produced some reaction in the other.

"Just let me have a ship, sir, ex officio. We could always *import* a few thousand bipeds."

"You know the transference of subject or colonial races from one planet to another is highly illegal," Terekomy said, keeping his voice detached so that the Ballistics-Beadle did not take fright.

"A lot of things take place that are illegal," Ibowitter said firmly. "Illegality can only be proved where the offence is detected. Now, sir, I have some valuable contacts on Starjj. . . ."

He paused and looked knowingly at Terekomy.

The latter said, "You have certain qualities that recommend you for promotion, Ibowitter. If the ability to keep quiet is among them, you may find yourself doing more interesting work in a few weeks. I will think of your suggestion, while you must forget it. Do these Starjj bipeds resemble Earth bipeds, by the way?"

"Very closely, sir. In all but a few minor details."

"Hm. Well, see that Rivars has undisturbed sleep tonight. That is all."

The automotor hummed him back down the fine road towards the palace. Terekomy was smiling under his arms. He thought he saw a way of helping the Commissioner. But the scheme, he determined, should be entirely his own.

The road over which he sped was a thread on the globe over which Par-Chavorlem, some of his staff officers, and Towler poured. They were choosing a site for the temporary Commission City that was to be no bigger than regulations allowed. Several officers had made sugestions pointing out various parts of the globe.

"No," said Par-Chavorlem at length, "I see no reason why we should unduly inconvenience ourselves by moving far from here, even for an inquisitive signatory. Nor do we wish to lose contact with Rivars' army."

He indicated a point along the escarpment at the edge of the Channel Valley.

"What about here? To the south of it was once a narrow and meaningless strip of sea. One of my more imaginative predecessors drained it. It might be pleasant to have a city within sight of such an enterprise. And two roads meet conveniently. There is a ruined city not far away which will not trouble us. It's native name is Eastbon. I see. Do you know anything about Eastbon, Interpreter?"

"It has some history in pre-Empire days," Towler said, speaking in Partussian.

"Right. Take a note, translate it into terrestial, get it up into Transmissions as soon as possible, see it is circulated to all native contractors concerned. Make it read: *Labour conscriptors and labourers are advised that work for four thousand hands will shortly become available in the region of Eastbon, convergence of Routes 2A and 43B. Tasks of up to a year's duration proposed. Standard contract all grades, less Native Improvement Levy.*"

He turned his back to his officers as Towler bowed and headed for the Transmissions Room. So the Commissioner had not only been out of the palace, but had taken to the air. It was almost unprecedented! Although some of the details remained obscure, already it was clear that something of the utmost importance was brewing.

On his way through the palace, Towler met Peter Lardening, the young interpreter. He put his hand out as if to detain Towler.

"Oh, Interpreter Towler, forgive me, but about Elizabeth Fallodon. Do you think –"

"I'm sorry. I mustn't stop," Towler said.

Even Elizabeth and her affairs must wait now.

But as he hurried into the interpreters' off-duty room to pick up an oxygen cylinder before running home, Lardening followed him in. Several of the other interpreters were there, smoking and talking: Reonachi, Meller, Johns and Wedman. They greeted the Chief Interpreter cheerfully.

"Start hammering, boys," he said, nodding to them.

Grinning, they leant against the sides of the room and commenced to beat them with palms or fists. The spy system in the City being what it was, they did not doubt that this room was wired. Consequently when they had anything important to say they beat the walls to set up vibrations which would baffle any concealed microphones. It was one way of annoying their conquerors.

"We're going to be moved out of this City, at least for a while," Towler said, speaking through the din. "Someone's evidently got news of what goes on here through to Partussy and we're going to be investigated. Chav is obviously unsettled.

All of you keep your ears open and pass on any details."

They cheered louder than they knocked, and then beseiged him with questions.

As soon as he was free to leave, Towler hurried back to his apartment. He did not bother to remove his air suit. After busying himself in the kitchen for some minutes, ignoring the unsleeping eye of the glimpse-globe, he took the meat he had purchased earlier back to the butcher. The butcher, who was about to close, eyed him suspiciously.

"I dislike complaining, but this cut is not of the freshest, butcher," Towler said. "I wish to return it."

After some haggling, the butcher took the cut back, threw it under the counter, and gave the interpreter another one. When his shop had closed, he wandered casually over to the counter and picked up the offending meat. His probing fingers soon discovered the plastic capsule Towler had inserted in it. It would contain a message. Tomorrow morning early, the capsule would pass to a refuse man whose job necessitated his leaving the City daily. From him, the chip would soon pass to the patriots' stronghold in the hills, and directly into the hands of Rivars.

Within twenty-four hours of its arrival on Earth, the preliminary announcement of Signatory Synvoret's proposed visit was causing a stir everywhere.

IV

The next two years, objective time, were crowded ones. As the Signatory made his long journey, stage by stage towards Earth, the various factions on that planet prepared to receive him, each in its different way.

For Synvoret and his party, the subjective time of the voyage was only four months. And at least half of that period was passed at spaceport hotels dotted across the universe, waiting to catch a connection headed in their desired direction. Even with a high priority ticket, it took the party five hops to reach Earth.

At the end of the fourth hop, grounded on a planet named Appelobetnees III, Synvoret was lucky. He was due to catch an Official Lines ship in two days which would take him to Earth via Castacorze. Then he learnt of a warp freighter leaving for Partussy via Saturn.

Synvoret summoned the freighter captain and quickly made his arrangements.

"Sure, I can put your party off on Earth and collect you on the way back from Saturn," the captain said. He was a heavily whiskered creature, tall as a nul, shaped like a shrimp. "Since we shall be in ordinary space for most of that intersystem hop, you should get eight or nine clear days on Earth. After which I will have you back in Partussy in eight weeks subjective time."

"Excellent," Synvoret said.

"Get aboard the *Geboraa* this evening, and we clear Appelobetnees III at ten chimes tomorrow."

"Excellent," Synvoret said again.

Before informing the rest of his party of this change of plans, he took a reflective turn around the spaceport.

It disturbed him to find how relieved he was to have a way home planned before he had reached his destination. Although he solaced his conscience by telling himself that nine days was ample to prove or disprove Par-Chavorlem's guilt, he could not so easily forget that only a short while ago he had been promising himself the longest possible time away from home.

"I'm getting old, missing my own hearth," he muttered.

Relieved, he began to go back to the hotel, simply reversing like a locomotive, instead of actually turning round like a man. As he skirted the spaceport barrier, a nul outside called to him. Swivelling an eye-stalk, Synvoret saw a ragged fellow detach himself from the multishaped crowd of passersby and come up to the fence, obviously attracted by the signatorial uniform. Synvoret halted agreeably.

"You have the bearing of a civilized nul," the ragged one said through the fence. "I'd lay ten to one you'll be off this accursed planet within a matter of hours. In the diplomatic service, are you not? So was I once. Now by a turn of fortune's wheel I rot on this rain-drenched mud ball."

"Out of work, eh?" Synvoret inquired guardedly, not keen to hear a long hard luck story.

"Not through my own fault, sir. Nor is it my fault I'm fleeced every *byaksis* I need to get away from this dump. I beg you, spare me nine tens."

Synvoret could be generous enough when the gift ensured the disappearance of an unwanted recipient.

"Here you are," he said, holding out the small coins. "But why ask for nine tens, instead of a whole hundred?"

The ragged nul raised his arms in the Partussian smile.

"I'm a gambler, sir. I'm gambling my way home across the universe. Nine tens happens to be the exact price of one Appelobetneesian lottery ticket. That's what I need! The prize money's almost enough to take me all the way to Partussy, and the odds of winning are said to be ninety-six million to one."

"It's not a chance I'd throw away nine tens on," Synvoret said.

"Ninety-six million happens to be my lucky number," the tattered nul said, rippling his comb and merging back into the crowd.

Shaking his head – partly with pleasure – at the foolishness of the nul, Synvoret returned to tell his retinue of their new departure time. Twenty hours later, they were in deep warp, boring for Earth.

On Earth, the interested parties were ready for him – just.

So cunning and determined was the armed opposition of the patriots under Rivars, that commencement of work on the new City at Eastbon was postponed for some weeks until Arm Marshall Terekomy's ground forces, hampered by orders to spill human blood as sparingly as possible, had performed mopping up operations. The new City began to rise, its modest volume calculated not to offend the tape measures of any suspicious investigators.

Then the native labour gangs engaged in its construction became difficult. A "go slow" policy lasted for three days until twelve bipeds taken at random were publicly disintegrated by stereosonus. Again the work proceeded slowly, but at last it was done. The first step to deceive Synvoret had been taken.

By leaving a strong rear party in the old City, which was now concealed from every eye behind negavision screens, Par-Chavorlem was able to bring the establishment he installed in the new City within the officially stipulated maximum numbers.

Terekomy had pressed energetically ahead with his no less sizeable task, which he still managed to keep secret from his superior. Ballastics-Beadle Ibowitter came to report the completion of his part of the scheme, tapping a map importantly against his flank as he entered Police HQ.

Presenting the map to Terekomy, he indicated two shaded areas on it.

"Here is where we believe the main body of Rivars' rebels to be concentrated, sir," he said. "And just *here* I have personally seen to the disposition of five thousand Starjjans, male and female – these bipeds have but two sexes, as you know, sir. They are in well-covered ground, with ample opportunities for defence and attack."

Terekomy was suddenly gloomy. With a flash of insight, he saw how a wish to please Par-Chavorlem had led him into a delicate position; to present his superior with this dangerous *fait accompli* might well bring him anger rather than congratulation.

"How did you get them off Starjj? Are you sure you weren't seen?"

"Absolutely, sir. I took three ships. We landed on the night tide and removed all the adult inhabitants of one hill town. They were somnalized. The whole thing went without hitch. I count it as my most successful operation to date."

Terekomy flapped his comb contemptuously.

"You should have brought me one of those alien bipeds to examine. How nearly do they resemble terrestial bipeds?"

"The differences are almost negligible. They possess a vestigial tail, webbed feet – acquatic origins, sir – and some slight modification in the sexual organs which need worry nobody. Any other questions, sir?"

At his unctuous mixture of insolence and servility, Terekomy allowed the inside of his comb to turn a faint viridian.

"You know why we've got these infernal creatures here, Ibowitter. To stage a good show for this visiting brass hat, to convince him Earth needs to be repressed by force. What makes you think they and the terrestials will fight?"

The Ballistics man raised an arm in the gentlest irony. He was a civilized nul, and had read much of the history of the two species he exterminated so efficiently.

"Your answer, sir, like most answers to most questions, lies in past history. One group of bipeds will fight any other group of bipeds. They have this natural law which is called, I believe, the Survival of the Fiercest."

"Dismissed, Ibowitter. Your services will be suitably rewarded. I know an aspiring nul when I see one."

Somewhat hurt by this abruptness, Ibowitter left the room, proceeded down the corridor, descended by the lift, turned towards the narrow front doors of the Police building. Before he reached them, three burly nuls seized him, one by each arm, removing him despite his protests to a subterranean cell. Next day his unfortunate death in a street accident was announced.

Directly after his final interview with Ibowitter, Terekomy went to Par-Chavorlem to announce, with the boldest face he could muster, his Starjjan scheme.

Par-Chavorlem received the news with mild interest.

He was feeling highly pleased with himself, and was positively looking forward to Synvoret's arrival on the morrow. He relished the art that had been lavished on the deception of this one nul. The truth was, Par-Chavorlem was an able administrator gone wrong; the desire and the capacity to regulate turns easily into a compulsion to manipulate. Pulling strings was Par-Chavorlem's joy; exploiting his victims but a by-product of that pleasure.

"These Starjjans," he said judiciously. "You are running a risk taking them off their native planet. Our history over the last million years shows the danger of allowing two subject races even the remotest chance of uniting together. Very strict laws have been framed to guard against this eventuality. If your ingenious move were ever discovered by the wrong person – Synvoret, let's say – I doubt if even our well-bribed friends on Castacorze could help us out."

Terekomy disliked hearing his own arguments brought against him.

"Nobody will find out. We came and went secretly. As for Starjjan and terrestial uniting! These imported wretches are on an alien planet, speaking an alien tongue. They will not be in diplomatic mood. Nor will Rivars. To him they will be invaders to be exterminated.

"I've seen to it that the Starjjans have been equipped with strong enough weapons to ensure that although their eventual defeat is inevitable, it will be protracted enough to give our visiting signatory and his boys the impression that a first-class civil war is raging here."

"You have contrived well," Par-Chavorlem said.

Terekomy's comb flushed with pleasure.

On what might be termed the domestic front, several significant changes had been made. Gary Towler found his interpreter's salary increased, as well as his off-duty hours. He observed that Par-Chavorlem made an obvious effort to be more polite to him when they met – even to the point where other men working about Commission City muttered of favouritism.

Towler bore it as well as possible. Against his growing unpopularity among the other interpreters he tried to set the unexpected advantages of living in the new City. Forced to curtail some of his more obviously sinister activities for the time, Par-Chavorlem had unwillingly given more freedom to the bipeds who worked in the City.

But nothing compensated for the growing coldness Elizabeth Fallodon showed Towler. In the past two years she had become resigned to her work and was even gay. She had put on weight, grown beautiful. In Towler's rather isolated life, she was the brightest thing. He shivered now to think she might try to avoid him.

On the eve of Synvoret's arrival, Towler returned early to his apartment. He had ceased to do his own shopping for dislike of being snubbed in the street. His supplies were now delivered to the flat.

He sat down to a solitary meal with much appetite. When he cut open his meat pie, he found a plastic capsule in it. Turning pale, he wiped it on his napkin and opened it.

The message was concise. It said he was to present himself at the butcher's shop at 1955 hours that evening, just before closing. Arrangements were made for him to be smuggled out of the Commission for a personal conference at the patriots' stronghold. He would be delivered safely back to the City before dawn to resume duties. The note was signed by Rivars, the now almost legendary name of the patriot leader.

Towler could eat no pie. His stomach jumped nervously as he destroyed the message. Fluttering around the room, he tried to regain control of himself. Nevertheless, the idea of not obeying did not enter his head. He knew the future of Earth might well rest in his reluctant hands.

When his doorbell buzzed, he went towards it trembling. He was expecting no one.

It was Elizabeth. This was beauty to him, this narrow face, with its gently long nose and a mouth in contrast: not cruel,

34

but predatory, demanding. The mouth and nose combined with her bright eyes to produce a unique, an individual countenance. He flattered himself to think that few could recognize as he did her special loveliness. The two years she had spent in Commission service had matured rather than crushed her.

"What could be nicer than this?" he exclaimed. "Elizabeth, come in. It's too long since you've been here."

"Five days," she said, smiling. He saw at once she was wary.

"Five days is far too long. Elizabeth, when I hear you at work having to talk in the cold, hard Partussian, you seem like another person – just as I'm another person when I'm with you. You must know how I –"

There was a tawny light in her eyes now. The shades in them changed with every mood.

"Please, Gary, don't say any more just now," she begged, breaking into his speech. "It only makes what I have to say more difficult." She paused, glancing up at the ceiling.

"Go ahead, go and say what you want," he said, almost roughly. "There are no private glimpse-globes in this new city, no spy system that we know of. Say anything!"

"I only wanted to say that we ought not to meet privately any more. Thank you for the coaching in Partussian you've given me."

"Why this? Why so sudden?"

"For no reason. . . . I just feel our interests are very different, that's all."

Towler was not one to persist or persuade; he could only aquiesce. Suddenly he wanted to be away, to save her having to deliver these little speeches which surely hurt her. He looked at her and his attitude minutely altered.

"Such as our interest in Peter Lardening?" he asked.

"How unlike you to say that!" She was stung.

"How do you know what's like or unlike me? Listen, Elizabeth, even when we're close together there is a barrier between us, isn't there? Well, it isn't my fault – I mean, the barrier is removable. You see, I'm always under a certain strain – you'd better know – I'm an agent for Rivars, passing information from the palace. I'm living constantly out on a limb."

He had not meant to tell her. His mind instantly went off in circles of recrimination, returning only partly to hear her say, "That alters so much for me. It's been difficult, Gary –"

35

Suddenly he caught hold of her, roughly swinging her towards him. At that she stopped talking. Anger kindled in her eyes as she pulled her arm away.

"You look just fine like that!" Towler exclaimed. "Elizabeth, why should I be afraid to speak out to you? You are very dear to me, partly because you often behave as I do."

"Oh, do I? How exactly?"

"How? You were planning to make a break with me because you've listened to the other interpreters instead of following your own instinct. You thought I was Chav's toady, didn't you? I don't *blame* you, Elizabeth, but you were thinking conventionally, just as I often do. We're both conventional people, caught now in an unconventional situation, and we must try to overcome it."

"Gary, you're so ... diffident." Her chin was still pugnacious. "Yes, I do like you. You've helped me so much, but you ought to be more *defiant* –"

"Just try and understand that both of us probably have a lot in our lives to work out. Your attraction is not only that you are conventional, as I am, but that there's a tiger buried in you, as there is in me. That's what's between us. That's why we need each other badly."

As Towler hurried to the butcher's, he reflected with some wonder on what he had said to Elizabeth. It cost him great effort to speak his mind unhampered to anyone, particularly to a woman. Only to Elizabeth had he revealed the secret feeling that had long possessed him; that given the moment he could rise to it from his shell. Now it seemed the moment was at hand – and he trembled.

When he presented himself at the butcher's, he was unceremoniously bundled under a counter out of sight. There he stayed until the shop was closed and the shutters put up. The butcher helped him to his feet.

"To think that you'll be speaking with Rivars in a couple of hours," he exclaimed. "The other city was too rigged with spy devices for anyone to slip in and out. But here it's another matter, while it lasts. It's a golden opportunity for you. I wish I were you."

Overawed by the thought of his mission, Towler merely grunted. The butcher, misinterpreting, thought he was being aloof.

"I am sorry we always have to treat you like an outcast,
36

sir," he said, brushing Towler down apologetically. "It breaks my heart to be discourteous to you, respecting you as I do. But orders are orders, and we never know who may be watching, do we, even in this city? You're a real hero, sir, and it's a pleasure to know you. Now if you'd just step into this refuse bin. . . ."

Clamping up the faceplate of his suit, Towler crouched uncomfortably in the bin, suffering a sack to be placed over his shoulders and rubbish to be poured on top of it. After only a brief wait, a disposal cart arrived at the back door, and Towler's bin was dumped unceremoniously on it. For half an hour they lumbered through the streets, collecting other refuse.

Finally they arrived at the "gate". Partussy sentries clumped round the cart, cursorily inspecting and passing it. A neutralizer was switched on, the force field died locally and they passed into the airlock tunnel. Two minutes later they were in the fresh Earth air with darkness round them.

At the tip, half a mile down the road, Towler's bin was unloaded, the refuse man helping him out. Towler stretched gratefully, dwarfed by the bulk of the atomic disposer.

"Now mister, you better get yourself moving," the man advised. "The force fields are broken here while I dump my load. Behind this tip you'll find one solitary tree. It marks the beginning of a path that'll take you into the beginning of Channel territory. Keep on down it fast as you can and someone will meet you. His challenge will be 'dry bread' and your answer wil be 'hot ice'. Got that? Okay then, off you go and all the best!"

Darkness was almost complete. The ill-defined path was not easily kept to. Towler did his best, a dizziness compiled of apprehension and elation in his veins. The air, thick as cream, seemed to pour through his being. He was in the open for the first time in ten years. For the first time in ten years stars gleamed overhead. Perhaps one day. . . .

The challenge was flung at him from the darkness.

"Dry bread!"

Startled, he gave the countersign and heard a safety catch click on.

A gaunt man appeared, little more than a dark outline against the lighter path. He beckoned Towler to follow almost without a word. They scrambled down a broken, chalky bank into a belt of high scrub, moving so fast and so far that Towler

37

almost cried for respite. Shuddering for breath, sweating under the atmosphere suit he still wore, he emerged behind the guide into a stony clearing. Two horses waited with another mounted man.

They rode in an easterly direction for over an hour. Towler had never ridden an animal. Every minute was an agony for him.

Their way was mainly downhill, through curiously broken territory. Once they passed by the fringe of a planted forest. When they trotted into a ravine, stopping before a row of huts sheltered under a crumbling cliff, Towler dismounted stiffly and looked about.

Rivar's temporary headquarters consisted of little more than a few tents and huts, as far as could be seen. Advantage had been taken of the natural cover afforded by the ravine, but the threat of discovery by nul reconnaisance forces was comparatively slight. Their aversion to air travel limited the number of their aircraft sorties, while their faith in their impregnable roads tended to make them disregard the waste areas between.

Tethering the horses, Towler's guides led him into one of the huts. Food and drink awaited him there, and he set to with gratitude, removing the helmet of his suit.

He was still eating when Rivars entered.

V

In these recessional days for Earth, Rivars was perhaps the only terrestial name known all over the globe. Other patriot leaders existed, scattered over the other continents, but none had ever survived before so close to the centre of nul rule. The very fact that Rivars pitted his wits and strength against the City itself had contributed to his power.

He was an average-sized man in his fifties, compactly built. In his full crop of black hair was one wide and startling streak of grey. He wore leather overalls, a long cloak, boots, and a round cloth hat. His eyes were steady and penetrating, their heavy lids giving him the hooded look of an eagle. Though he entered the hut without ceremony, the air of authority about him was such that Towler dropped his fork and rose.

38

Motioning him to sit again, Rivars took the chair beside him and faced him.

"I appreciate your coming, Towler," he said. "I am aware of the risks you take in being here, but a personal discussion is necessary between us, and fortunately the lack of police refinements in the new Commission make it possible."

Without further preface, he began to talk about the arrival of Signatory Synvoret, now only a few hours ahead.

"Your notes to us have kept us informed of what happens at the palace, but I wish to see that I have the significance of this visit clear. First then, the Colony Worlds Council of Partussy expect the exploitation of subject planets like Earth, but this exploitation is rigorously limited by charter. Right?"

"That is correct," Towler agreed. "Naturally they call it development rather than exploitation."

"And Par-Chavorlem is exceeding the exploitation limit and breaking his charter?"

A tight, grim smile passed between them as Towler again said, "That is correct."

"Good. The benefits of this exploitation go into the pockets of Par-Chavorlem, his friends, and those contacts whose silence he finds it necessary to purchase. Right?"

"Quite right."

"And this corruption must undoubtedly extend to his immediate superiors at GAS Vermilion HQ Castacorze?"

"We have no direct proof of this, sir, but it must be so. As you know, inspecting bodies from Castacorze have visited Earth from time to time, and nothing has changed. Someone powerful there must be bought, or Par-Chavorlem would have been out of office long ago."

Rivars sat silent a full minute, digesting this. Finally he said, "Since I am little more than a rebel captain, this question can be merely of academic interest. But why would you say such graft exists in the middle of an energetic empire?"

It was not an easy question.

"It is hard to gather information about what happens elsewhere in the galaxy," Towler said. "But I think what is happening on Earth may be fairly typical of other so-called Colonial Planets. In essence, the vast Partussian administrative system is going soft. Although it's too early to say yet, it may be that the old Empire is entering its decadent stage."

"I see. If that were so, a few healthy insurrections on a dozen planets like Earth might hasten the decline?"

"They might indeed, sir."

Rivars smiled the cold smile of a condor and said nothing. In his mind was a clear little picture of worlds exploding like bullets.

Unexpectedly, he reached out and snapped off the light. He walked towards the window, grunting to Towler to follow. There, taking a torch from under his cloak, he shone it into the night.

The beam picked out the opposing cliff, creating it suddenly from the darkness in all its detail of embossed stone and hanging grass. At its top, a ragged spar projected almost vertically into the air.

"There's a symbol for you, Towler. That's the mast of an old ship. It must be twelve hundred years old at least. All this area used to be sea bed just a few centuries ago. That ship sunk through a series of accidents; now it's been raised up again through another series. The same thing will happen to Earth. Our job is to engineer the right accidents."

The demonstration was, Towler thought, ingenious. Reproaching himself for lack of loyalty, he still could not see the need for it. He blinked embarrassedly as the light came on and they resumed their seats. As if to counter a weak moment of romanticism, Rivars' voice was matter-of-fact sounding when he spoke again.

"Now for the main business of our discussion. The visit of this Signatory Synvoret is obviously vital to us all. It may be the only time that someone with almost complete power, a member, in fact, of the Colony Worlds Council itself, comes personally to Earth within the next five centuries. Tell me, would it be possible for Par-Chavorlem to bribe Synvoret?"

Towler hesitated. Rivars poured him some wine which he drank almost without noticing.

"You realize, sir," he said at length, "that if Synvoret discovers the true state of affairs on Earth Par-Chavorlem will be a broken man. The result will undoubtedly be justice and restitution for our people. I believe Synvoret, who is disinterested and has a high reputation, to be incorruptible. And I believe Par-Chavorlem knows he is incorruptible. Hence all the subterfuges he has been preparing for these past two years."

The patriot leader stood up, letting his chair fall backwards.

Eyes gleaming, he took a turn about the hut. As he walked, he punched a fist into his other palm.

"Then we shall win through at last, Towler! All our sacrifices will not have been in vain. If we cannot acquaint this honest man with the truth of our position, then we do not deserve the smell of freedom."

They had been in accord until now, two men filled with the same aspirations. The tensions of the night, the murmuring voices of the guards outside, the food cooling on the table were forgotten by Towler as he talked to this leader in whom everyone's faith was limitless. He had felt himself for once at the centre of things, near the core of truth.

Suddenly, Rivars' exultant words cracked Towler's faith from top to bottom. He found himself on the edge of an abyss of doubt. Only of one thing was he sure: Rivars was naïve.

It was understandable enough. Rivars was a fighter, a leader. He knew the ways of soldiers and the tactics of generals. With the lay of the country and the taste of adversity he was more than familiar. But of the cunning of diplomats he comprehended nothing.

Towler had been forced to live among diplomats. He knew that bribery was only one weapon in Par-Chavorlem's arsenal. He guessed that the Commissioner would have a dozen ways of winning Synvoret's silence.

He rose to speak, to protest, to state what was on his mind. The leader clapped him on the shoulder and proposed a toast to forthcoming freedom, snatching up the wine as he did so.

"I will see that proof of corruption gets before Signatory Synvoret! The way is clear!" he exclaimed. In that horrible moment, Towler saw that the future of Earth might rest not on Rivars' broad shoulders but on his own reluctant ones. Rivars did not know what he was dealing with.

Turning his face away, he sipped the wine. "The situation may be more complex than you imagine, sir. In any case, whatever evidence we place in Synvoret's hands must be foolproof and tangible. Documents are hardly enough. They may convince Synvoret, but when taken halfway across the galaxy they will not convince the Colony Council."

"I understand. We will deal with that in a moment," Rivars said, rather curtly.

Silence fell. They heard a man laugh some distance from the hut.

"My friend, you still have an important part to play in our affairs," Rivars said, glancing at his watch. "The time nears for you to ride back to the City, so I will be brief. I must tell you, as you may have suspected, that I have other sources of information than you close to Par-Chavorlem, although none so close or so valued as you. This is partly to ensure I am not left absolutely uninformed if anything happens to you, you understand."

In fact, Towler had guessed as much, although to have his guess confirmed piqued his pride. It meant he was not quite as valuable as Rivars claimed. He said merely, "This is one of the advantages of having an enemy foolish and arrogant enough to refuse to learn their victim's language. It makes them dependent on a number of victims."

Rivars laughed shortly, as if he had not considered that aspect before.

"My sources tell me," Rivars continued, "that the promotion and better treatment you have enjoyed recently is because Par-Chavorlem plans to use you as Synvoret's personal interpreter. He will not try to bribe Synvoret. He will bribe *you* to give Synvoret his version of the facts. On *you* will rest the onus of convincing Synvoret that all is well on Earth."

His heart sinking again, Towler said numbly, "I had almost suspected as much."

Rivars stared him straight in the eyes.

"Par-Chavorlem's offer to you will be considerable."

The interpreter kept his face wooden. Irritation filled him to think that this man who had unknowingly just failed his crucial test was now testing him. When the silence had extended itself until it seemed to fill all memory, he said, "I am an Earthman, leader. I know where my loyalties lie."

"We too have the power to make offers," Rivars said, speaking rather quickly. "If we manage our affairs properly in the next week, freedom lies ahead of us. Your services will not go forgotten, Towler. You shall have ten acres of land and a house built for you overlooking the sea. You will not have to work again, once we are free from this regime."

Again Towler felt exasperation, knowing that these promises only signified that Rivars was unsure of him, did not know how much to trust him. He stood up.

"Give me my instructions," he said harshly. "I will see they are carried out."

42

"Sit down with me, drink some more wine," Rivars said and, when they were seated, continued. "We must provide Synvoret with material proof of the true state of affairs here on Earth. As you say, copies of documents will mean little on Partussy. The Signatory must take back with him some simple, tangible, dramatic piece of evidence to show conclusively that Par-Chavorlem is overstepping his powers here. If we can do just that, Earth should be freed from his tyranny."

Towler looked sceptical.

"What sort of evidence have you in mind?"

He fancied that uncertainty flickered across the hard face opposite him.

"I will find something," Rivars said smoothly, "and I will see that it reaches you within three days. Your part, your vital part, in this will be to present Synvoret with that evidence when a suitable opportunity occurs. Until that opportunity occurs, in order to raise no suspicions, it is essential that you play the part Par-Chavorlem allots you. Afterwards, of course, you must answer straightly any questions the Signatory may ask you. Is this all clear, Gary Towler?"

The interpreter looked down at his fingers. Suddenly he felt very tired.

"I will do as you instruct. You may depend on me."

Rivars rose and shook his hand.

"Earth depends on you," he said solemnly. "You will not let us down."

Towler picked his helmet off the table and together they went out into the cold night. A slender moon had risen and Towler, hands in pockets, stood numbly surveying the scene. In the ravine, men in fur-trimmed coats were moving rapidly here and there. He caught the gleam of atomic arms, those pathetically outdated terrestial weapons ineffective against the force fields of the Partussians. He heard orders, quietly given but ringing like metal in his ears as the ravine walls buffeted them back. All these men moved united in a common cause. Yet for Towler this was a chill moment of isolation. He knew he was no man of action. The thought of the tension he would have to endure for the next few days left him limp.

"It has been a privilege to come and see you," he said formally.

"I am happy that Par-Chavorlem's present weakness permitted it," Rivars said. "No doubt he'll be glad to get back to the greater security of his original city. Is that closed down now?"

"A skeleton staff keeps it running. A convoy takes orders and supplies there every dawn. It's appalling to think we'll be back there, spied on every moment, before the month's out."

"It will not be for long," Rivars said resoundingly, as Towler's two guides came up with the horses.

As Towler reluctantly mounted, a runner came panting up to Rivars. "A Starjian force estimated at two hundred men reported from our outpost at Beaker's Hill, decamping, moving east north east towards the Varne Heights."

"I'll come," Rivars said. Breaking into a rapid walk, he vanished into the night. He had dismissed Towler from his mind.

"Let's get moving," one of the guides said.

They retracted their steps, riding at good speed through the moonlight. The journey was without incident. Despite his discomfort and tiredness, Towler even found pleasure in the great, mysterious land about him, in the dark trees beneath which they passed, in the subtle differences of temperature between hilltops, and hollows, in the great dome of the firmament floating unsupported above them.

At the rubbish tip, an empty refuse cart awaited him. For concealment, Towler was forced into the tool box beneath the driver's seat. In frantic discomfort, he was bumped back into the Commission, lying with his heart thumping as they stopped at the gate for the guard's search. At last they rolled forward again, into captivity.

It was still dark when Towler regained his room, sick with apprehension lest his absence had been detected. But everything was normal; the blank square of walls, the dark and battered armchair, the never-failing heat control, the shadowless light burning overhead. There in that static isolation he felt safe again.

Face down on his bed, he slept while the sun rose, was still sleeping when the freighter *Geboraa* touched down on Earth with Synvoret aboard.

VI

Almost everything was ready. The preparations for Synvoret's
visit had affected every man and nul in Commission City.
Now the community waited, with various degrees of confidence
or apprehension, as Par-Chavorlem prepared to put his colossal bluff into action and pose as a just man.

Outside the city, too, the effects of the visit were already
being felt. On several estates, at lumber camps, in Sub-Commissions, on *afrizzian* ranches, and at other places where the
Signatory was due to call or stop for an inspection, an un-
natural preparedness formed like ice.

And at about the same time as Synvoret's ship, *Geboraa*,
grounded, Rivars' rebels launched their first attack against the
encroaching Starjjans and were repulsed with heavy casualties.

Signatory Armajo Synvoret disembarked on Earth in a determined mood. He had covered half a galaxy and the last two
objective years mainly in *jarm*, a trance-state practised by high
caste Partussy officials. As a result, his mind was revitalized and
his will to see justice done increased tenfold.

As soon as his ship touched down on the spaceport, the force
field rolled in overhead, and in ten minutes the enclosed air
was fit for nuls to breathe. The main port of the ship rolled
open. Synvoret descended the steps as banners waved and a
robot band unit played. Very few Partussians were present to
greet him. Synvoret noted the fact.

His entourage consisted of only four nuls: a valet; a young
secretary being groomed for better things; a strong-armed and
inarticulate bodyguard named Raggball; and a senior member of the Psycho-Watch Branch, Gazer Roifullery. By the
time these nuls arrived home again, their combined travelling
and additional expenses would cost the Greater Partussian
Government something like a megabillion *byaksis*. Here lay
one of the prime reasons for corruption in the outer fringes of
empire. The financial reason, the cost of sending impartial
investigators to any outlying planet was colossal.

Synvoret arrived determined to find any corruption that
might exist. He was aware that Supreme Councillor Graylix's

main motive in sending him here had been to humour him. It placed him under an obligation which he could remove by proving Par-Chavorlem's guilt.

But from the first moment of his arrival, the business of lulling his suspicions went smoothly under way. The small reception committee which greeted him at the spaceport consisted of Par-Chavorlem himself, Arm Marshall Terekomy and three under-officers, as well as a small body of nul civilians, one of whom read a brief speech of welcome. The speech was a cunning mixture of the usual phrases concerning aspirations, achievements and nul destiny. When this cermony was over, the civilians came to clasp arms with Synvoret and mouth the age-old platitudes concerning the comfort of the Signatory's journey. All went as Par-Chavorlem had rehearsed it, reckoning that to bore Synvoret was in part at least to reassure him.

Par-Chavorlem himself, drawing his illustrious visitor aside, was careful not to be too obsequious. His role was that of a harassed commander, good at heart, but too burdened by the responsibilities of a rebellious planet to have much time for courtesy. Accordingly, the escorts bundled into a worn Army truck, while Par-Chavorlem led the Signatory and Gazer Roifullery to a road-flier of the type generally used for freight duties.

"Forgive this inhospitable vehicle, Signatory," Par-Chavorlem said apologetically. "During the emergency, any transport has to be pressed into duty. We have little in the way of luxury on Earth. I only hope we can make your stay here sufficiently comfortable. I'm sure that on Partussy –"

"I can do without luxury," Synvoret said.

They sped down one of the beautiful roads, under the misty arch of force, the landscape only a blur. As they went, both nuls were trying to sum each other up. Perhaps feeling some of that sinister charm which attracted Terekomy, Synvoret wondered which of the sexes Par-Chavorlem was. The sex – male, female or neuter – of a nul was not externally apparent, nor was it ever revealed except to the other potential participants in a mating trio. Nuls, especially the original Partussian stock, were reticent in everything, and never more so than in this matter.

The spaceport was only a short way from the City. Soon they had arrived, and were sliding through the gates. At once the City enclosed them, the City was the whole world. And it was a Partussian world. Replicas of this City existed all over the galaxy, all virtually identical, no matter the nature of the planet outside. Partussians did not adapt to the native environment, preferring to carry their own environment with them.

Synvoret looked around with interest and some dismay. The days of his Starjjan and other Commissionerships were long gone. He had forgotten how spartan these special cities were on unbreathable, lower class planets. Most of the buildings, besides being unabashedly utilitarian, were standardized and prefabricated. Par-Chavorlem had decided to take his guests on a tour of the city. This they now made, the Commissioner muttering a word of information now and again.

The gauntness of everything was emphasized by a lack of paint. Gazer Roifullery, the P-WB man, made a polite enquiry about the point.

"Unfortunately rebel guns shot down one of our supply craft as it was coming in to port," Par-Chavorlem said, inwardly relishing the smoothness with which he could lie. "They are rather vulnerable to attack while hovering above the port before the force fields close over them. In this instance, the craft luckily contained nothing more than five thousand gallons of paint."

"You should indent for more," Synvoret said mildly. "If you will forgive an old-fashioned remark, the brighter colour will improve the spirits of your citizens. Partussians are traditionally colour-loving people."

"We have more to worry about here than paint, sir," Par-Chavorlem said brusquely. He was not without sensitivity where the feelings of his own race were concerned. Much of his success on Earth was due to the gentle exploitation of the characters of those about him. Marshall Terekomy, for one. Now he was gauging and testing the nature of this man who was potentially his enemy, and acting in harmony with that judgement. Already his opinion was forming. He fancied Synvoret might prove a bluff and honest fellow possessing perhaps more crankiness than subtlety, who would interpret a little brusqueness as the candour of a sorely tried campaigner.

Few people were about, as they drove through the streets to the palace, and those either Partussian semi-leisured class or terrestial workers. Some of the former waved as the two vehicles swept past.

"What is the population of the City, Commissioner?"

Synvoret enquired. He knew by heart the figures laid down in the Statutes as maximum allowed to run a 5c colony like Earth: 150 Senior Grades, 1,800 Lower Grades, 200 Military, 2,000 Native All Grades, and 4,500 Dependants Total All Grades. Grand Overall Total 8,650.

"At present, we are some ten thousand strong, Signatory. We are generally under strength, but at present we also have to accommodate an armoured brigade sent from Vermilion HQ Castacorze to contain the native civil war, as well as some refugees from sub-commissions."

Synvoret remembered the difficulty of keeping open sub-commissions in time of trouble. A sub-commission was in practice merely the name of any town or village of a colonial planet where one or more nul administrators happened to be. They were rarely fortified, and the presence of the administrators often made them the focal point of local troublemakers.

"I shall be interested to acquire the local picture in detail," Synvoret said. "The record as it exists on the Queen Planet is naturally likely to be out of date in several respects."

"After a small luncheon we are holding for you, a complete briefing session has been arranged," said Par-Chavorlem.

"Thank you. That should help me in assessing the situation when I speak to local observers."

Noting the stiffness in the other's voice, the Commissioner answered in kind.

"That you will be able to do from tomorrow, when I shall assign you a terrestrial interpreter. Until then no official programme has been arranged. We presumed you might wish to rest after your long journey."

"I am not fond of official programmes," was all Synvoret said.

The luncheon at the palace was frugal. Plain fare carefully cooked was served, with cheap Partussy-type wines in support. Par-Chavorlem reflected cheerfully that the affront done to his palace was more than compensated by the disappointment his guest showed in the sparseness of the table.

"I trust you were adequately fed on the ships which brought you here?" he asked, tucking another mouthful of food under his arm.

"I was in *jarm* most of the time."

"Ah, a hungry business!"

After the meal, as Par-Chavorlem had announced, the briefing was held.

A team of grey-combed civilian experts reinforced their lectures with solids and steromaps. They were thorough. They talked at Synvoret and Roifullery for over two hours, giving them a suitably false picture of Earth's affairs, aiming to convince them, among other things, that a planet whose tribes indulged in civil war was not oppressed. Otherwise, why did the tribes not unite against the conqueror?

Par-Chavorlem did not sit through it. He marched out, impatient and nervous. Now the business of deception was under way, he was keen to get it over as soon as possible. He rang Terekomy on the private glimpse-globe.

"Have you asked the retinue when Synvoret leaves?"

"The frighter *Geboraa* returns from Saturn in eight or nine days, depending on the state of the spacelane through the asteroid belt. It departs after ten hours for re-fuelling and maintenance."

"Better than we dared hope for. I feared we might have him around our necks for months."

Terekomy twitched an eye-stalk encouragingly.

"Don't worry, Chavorlem. We'll soon have this old fool wrapped up. I've several little tricks to try on him."

"Just be careful," Par-Chavorlem said sharply. "Don't overstep the mark. You know I'm not entirely happy about this Starjj business. You heard him tell me at lunch he was actually on Starjj himself. Do nothing without consulting me."

He switched off.

This was really a game of bluff and double-bluff between him and his distinguished visitor. If Synvoret should discover any irregularities in the conduct of the Commission, he could – if he felt so disposed – make enough of them when he returned to Partussy to cost Par-Chavorlem his job. Charm must be used, as well as deception. But to what kind of charm would the leathery old diplomat be most susceptible?

He walked about his private room, his trained mind for the moment unfocussed. How did Synvoret tick? ... And from there, how did anyone tick? The galaxy swarmed with ticking creatures, the rulers and the ruled, their forms many and ingenious. But nobody could give you an answer to the mighty "why" of them. This problem had teased Par-Chavorlem since childhood, as another may be teased by a sexual problem.

On a table stood a bowl of Earth's flowers, pentstemons and marigolds mixed, a transplex dome over them to retard their death in the Partussian air. Snatching up a dazzling scarlet pentstemon, Par-Chavorlem pulled it and daintily crushed it. It was living, it had lived. Purpose? Meaning? Reason? In his flexed palm, crumpled petals could not answer.

He pounded on a bell.

Terrestial flowers were all display – like terrestial men. It was not so with Partussian flowers or with nuls. A Partussian flower resembled a stone, all its intricate and attractive parts hidden away. A Partussian concealed all his features except his eyes under the folds of his arms, where none but a lover might ever discover them.

One of his servants appeared in response to his ring, a young terrestial girl dressed in the olive green air suit that denoted service.

"Come here, Clotilda," Par-Chavorlem demanded. "Recite to me one of your poems in your native tongue while I watch you."

"Not again, sir," she begged.

"Yes, again, I command it."

He loomed over her, twice her height. Timorously, hopelessly, she began to recite in the language he would never understand. Snatching her up effortlessly, he peered at her, two swivelled eye-stalks close to the glass of her helmet.

She babbled, he did not listen. In strained intensity he stared through the separating glass, drinking in the movements of her jaw, chin, eyes, lips, mouth, tongue. These things should be hidden away in all but the ultimate situation. Yet here was a life-form, this flimsy, hateful, biped lifeform, flaunting the bright moving bits of itself. It was obscene, revolting. Yet Par-Chavorlem could not tear himself from the sight.

Only when the girl wept and struggled, and he had fed himself on the sight of her tears, did the Commissioner for Earth release her. These creatures did not always escape so lightly, but now he had other things on his mind. In particular, he knew he must speak cunningly to Towler.

VII

The briefing was at last over, the last question asked, the last answer given. The grey-combed lecturers put down their pointers and rolled up their maps. Signatory Synvoret and Gazer Roifullery returned to their private suite together.

"An admirably thorough briefing," commented the latter, who had taken tapes of the whole meeting.

"Thorough almost to the point of tedium," agreed Synvoret.

Tactfully reproving what seemed to him a superficial reply, Roifullery continued, "I was given an insight into bipedal life I never had before."

"I wasn't," Synvoret said dryly. "I received only a tripedal view of bipedal life. It is not enough to say that whereas Partussians never had nations and wars the terrestials always had and always will have. Consider the different planets we evolved on. On Partussy: no great temperature extremes, no impassable mountain ranges, sluggish rivers which were highways rather than barriers, and above all, no dividing seas. The reasons why we have never been nationalistic, you see, are physical rather than psychological.

"It may be for this same reason that a biped is a more complex creature than we are."

Roifullery's comb rippled at this heresy, but he said nothing, contenting himself with reflecting that those who think themselves simple may well be right.

"Our comparative simplicity," Synvoret continued, "has led us into a position of domination over all discovered biped species in the galaxy. This is not to say we should feel the lack of . . . respect for them I detected in that lecture room."

To this also Roifullery made no reply. He felt that his superior had come to Earth determined to find fault. It was not an objective attitude. It would need handling carefully. He sighed, but silently.

The Signatory went to his suite with no intention of resting. For perhaps five minutes he relaxed into a *jarm* posture. Then he changed into a less conspicuous uniform and went to find his own way out of the palace, Raggball his bodyguard following at a distance.

He emerged from a side door into a quiet courtyard, standing there for a moment to look up at the viridian sheen of the field above his head. Then he walked across the courtyard to the gate. The guard at the gate recognized Synvoret, saluted, and let them through.

Directly they were out of sight of the palace, Synvoret halted at the street corner. The bodyguard stopped obediently two paces behind him.

He had come to Earth meaning to get his facts straight from the horse's mouth. What he most wanted was to talk with one of the natives, although he realized from long experience that whatever a Commission native might say was unlikely to prove typical of opinion outside the Commission. Nevertheless, it would have its own value, if only as a standard for comparison. The few people on the street were Partussians, many of them moving with the briskness of those coming off or on to duty. Synvoret ignored them.

The whole scene was watched by Arm Marshall Terekomy from a room in Police HQ. By punching a series of buttons, he could throw on to a screen before him telepictures of various strategic points of the Commission's street system. This was one aid to subordination neither Par-Chavorlem nor Terekomy had dared to give up when they built the new city. The elaborate spy system in every private room had had to go – that useful illegality would have betrayed the regime for what it was to any hostile enquirer – but a few public peep holes were deemed essential to order.

The coloured images of Synvoret and his bodyguard showed clearly on the screen.

Terekomy raised his arms slightly.

"Eager beaver," he commented to his aide. "Out native hunting, if I know my diplomats. Well, he shall have one."

He crossed to the adjoining room, a branch of the radio station. Here a live schematic on the wall represented a diagram of the city, its moving lights indicating the whereabouts of those Partussians and terrestials who were Terekomy's "shadow column."

Identifying one of these lights with its individual number, Teremomy dialled it on the radio phone and began speaking at once.

"Calling you, E336. Listen in. Code Topstar and one fol-
lower are standing at the corner of Essrep and Fandandal. You
are nearest shadow to them. Proceed to them, engage them as
briefed. Make it good. I'll be listening! Out."

Terekomy returned to the screen in the other room.

In but a few seconds, a terrestial rounded the corner, nearly
blundering into Signatory Synvoret.

"I'm afraid we Partussians take up a lot of room," the
Signatory said, speaking to him at once. "It's an odd law of
the universe that tripeds always seem to have at least twice
the bulk of bipeds. I suppose, by the way, you understand and
speak Partussian?"

"Of course," the Earthman replied with a hint of irritation.
"It is a mark of culture to be able to speak your tongue, so
vastly more elaborate is it than my own."

"I see. You admire Partussian culture then?"

"Are you a stranger here by any chance, sir?"

"It happens that I am. This is my first visit to Earth,"
said the Signatory.

"Very interesting, sir. Then you can hardly know the intense
competition that we bipeds undergo for the privilege of serving
in your wonderful Commission City, and so being in contact
with a real civilization."

"Don't you find it irksome to be enclosed in that air suit
for most of the time you are in the City?"

"Even heaven must have its disadvantages, sir."

And with that the terrestial nodded cordially and passed on.
The Signatory made no attempt to analyse the conversation.
He was almost wholly dazed by the biped's face. This was
the first time for many years he had seen these creatures closely
other than in photostats. He recognized the shock he was
undergoing. It was chiefly a moral shock. These terrestials had
their private features, their mouths and other orifices, promin-
ently on display, in a manner distasteful to him. His reaction, in
short, was a limited, egocentric one. "I'm out of training," he
said to himself gloomily. "I'm getting old. Perhaps I ought
never to have come here. But how obscene their faces are."

Ignoring Raggball, he walked heavily back to the palace
and shut himself in his suite, ignoring even Roifullery.

For the first time, he felt fully his burden of responsibility. He
had come to find out the truth. But truth was notoriously an elu-
sive thing; on all the four million planets they had colonized,

the Partussy had found only local variants of it. In a complex universe, truth like time might be both subjective and objective, with no reconciliation possible between them. Suddenly the Signatory was lonely and homesick; he fancied that the air even here in the heart of the Commission was tainted with the beastly smell of oxygen.

All that evening he kept unsociably to his rooms. Par-Chavorlem was far from displeased with this. He had not dared to wire the Signatorial Suite, but hoped that his distinguished visitor might perhaps be feeling homesick. Synvoret's homesickness passed, however, as his analytical brain got to work.

His capacious, *jarm*-trained memory played him back word for word the brief conversation he had had with the terrestial outside. He had no means of judging empirically, but intuitively he fancied the thing was a little forced. Some of the biped's phrases hardly rang true, even allowing the fact that it had been speaking a language not its own. "Even heaven must have its disadvantages." How pat that was! And the phrase "we bipeds", would the member of an isolated 5c culture ever refer to itself in such a way? No, no, something phoney there.

Its arrival too. The only terrestial about, arriving suddenly and as hastily as if ordered to the spot. And its departure. As if, belying all it said, it was glad to beat a retreat. Or could he be imagining too much?

Raising himself on one flange, Synvoret called in Gazer Roifullery for a conference.

Par-Chavorlem was calling a conference at roughly the same time. Gary Towler sat primly before him in a chair that looked like a doll's chair compared with the one the Commissioner used.

"We have known each other ever since I came to Earth," Par-Chavorlem said to his chief interpreter. "I feel we know each other well, as far as that is possible between alien races. No doubt you realize how I have always tried to do my best for your somewhat recalcitrant peoples. Now that best has been questioned.

"I tell you this in confidence, Gary Towler, that the Signatory who is visiting us has come on a tour of inspection determined to prove that there is widespread corruption under my command. This Signatory, Synvoret, is merely a pawn of Partussian high politics, which seeks to replace me with one of their number, a dictator who will inevitably crush Earth and all its peoples."

So that was to be Chav's ostensible attitude! Towler reflected. In a word, keep me here or you'll get someone worse. The threat was blunt, yet the line of approach was subtle enough. He nodded submissively, continuing to listen.

"You can see then, Gary Towler, that we have in our midst a threat to your future as well as mine. With your help, it can be met."

"I am only a member of a subject race, sir."

"With your help it can be met, I say. You are my chief interpreter. You are going to be personally attached to the Signatory for the duration of his stay."

"It will be an honour," Towler said, reflecting that a lie to an alien diplomat was a service to Earth.

"An honour, yes, and a grave duty, which will not go unrewarded. Affairs at present are unsettled here. You speak Partussian like one of us. The Signatory naturally speaks no Earthian dialect. In his contacts with all natives, he will consequently be in your hands. You must see to it that he hears no opinions that are ill-informed or spiteful, or lack understanding of the difficulties with which I have to cope. Anything that may be called prejudicial against our present regime must not reach Synvoret's ears. In short, you must be interpreter *and* censor. Is this perfectly clear?"

"Very clear, sir. If a native says 'All our metal is exported', I translate this to the Signatory as 'None of our metal is exported'."

The comb on Par-Chavorlem's turret head rustled. He stood up.

"See you are subtle about it, Gary Towler," he said, towering over the Earthian. "I make you no threats, but you will be carefully watched."

"I understand."

"Excellent. One of Arm Marshall Terekomy's officers will brief you thoroughly on what is required after you leave here, and you will report to the Signatory in the morning. Understood?"

Towler stood up and nodded.

"Will that be all, sir?"

"No." The wide arms stretched out imperiously. "A further thing, and here I speak more personally. No terrestial has

55

ever been to Partussy the Queen Planet itself. If this impertinent visit passes successfully, I swear to you that you shall go to there afterwards, taking with you whom you will for company. Many oxygen-breathers live there in specially constructed cities. You would be comfortable. What is more, you would be famous. As the only terrestial, you could name your own price on threedee, dreemee or freak – er, personality shows. And, which would appeal to your altruistic nature more, you would be your planet's ambassador, able to speak freely in its favour. And if Partussy does not appeal, you and your companion can go to any Earth-type planet you care to name, without strings attached. Go away and think about this well."

Towler bit his lip. Here was the offer that Rivars had predicted Par-Chavorlem would make. It was, as predicted, considerable. Compared with the patriot leader's offer of ten acres and a house, it was more than considerable. The mere promise of a journey half across the galaxy was enough to dizzy a temperament like Towler's.

Never for a minute had the little interpreter considered making a bargain with Par-Chavorlem. Yet just to hear his offer brought sudden pleasure. It showed him how, even at his age, new doors might magically open. And if Elizabeth would go with him through those doors. . . .

He left the room shakily, the burst of pleasure fading. His path seemed no longer clear cut. The moral confusion in his mind was painful. Yet rather than try to clear it, he superimposed on it one question: could he not serve both Rivars and himself? Would not, in other words, some way present itself whereby he could give Synvoret Rivars' piece of evidence – whatever that was and whenever it came – without Par-Chavorlem's learning that he had done so?

Desperately, Towler needed to think. Before going to see Terekomy for briefing on what was to be said to the Signatory, he turned into the interpreters' off-duty room, taking off his helmet as he came through the airlock into it.

Silence fell.

Four people turned to survey his entry, suddenly stopping their conversation for it. Confused, Towler also paused, then went towards them. They were Elizabeth, Lardening, Chettle and Wedman, the latter two being generally attached to Palace Police.

Only Elizabeth smiled at Towler. She asked simply, "What's going to happen?"

"Chav has appointed me the interpreter to be attached to Synvoret during his visit," he said.

Chettle grunted. Their reaction was hostile but without surprise.

"Then you should get the chance to tell Synvoret how bad things really are here," Wedman said.

"It may be difficult to get him alone. You know we'll be watched," Towler said, almost to himself. The words, casually spoken, brought Chettle up close to him. Cy Chettle was a little, dark man with hairy fists, one of which he brought up to Towler's chest now.

"Listen, Gary, this week is our one big chance and we aren't going to mess it up. If you haven't got the guts to let this Synvoret know what goes on, bring him in here and *we'll* tell him. The big brass would soon boot out Chav if they found he was a dangerous fanatic."

Towler stepped back a pace, his face grim.

"Get your facts right, Cy. Chav's *not* a fanatic. Fanaticism burns itself out. Chav will never tire. Cruelty, extortion, oppression, they're not a way of life to him, they're a hobby. That's why he's more dangerous than you realize."

"If you feel like that, what are you waiting for?" Lardening asked, more curiosity than anger in his voice.

"Because he *is* dangerous, because we are being watched, because the situation is more subtle than you know."

He should not have said that. The subtlety chiefly existed in his own personal situation. Yet it silenced them all except Elizabeth.

"I don't see the subtlety, Gary," she said. "The position is clear enough. Synvoret must get the facts that Chav is trying to hide. Chav's getting worse every day. He nearly killed Clotilda early this afternoon. Yesterday one of the computer girls disappeared and it looks as if he took her."

Peter Lardening took gentle hold of her upper arm.

"I'll speak to Synvoret myself," he said. "I'm not afraid of any nul."

"Nor am I," Towler said in a choking voice, moving forward.

"Then why don't you prove it?" Lardening said, almost in a whisper. They were all rigid, Elizabeth staring fixedly at

Towler. He clenched his fist and raised it. Lardening knocked it contemptuously down with an open hand.

"Go to hell, Towler," he said, "but see you fix Synvoret first." He started for the airlock door, Chettle and Wedman picking up their breathing helmets and following him. "Don't you see, you fools," Towler shouted at their backs. "We don't have to do a thing. This Synvoret will find out how the wind blows for himself."

Lardening turned and beckoned to Elizabeth.

"Come on," he said impatiently.

"I think I'll stay here," she said.

The door slammed and she was alone with Towler.

Towler seized her wrists, tears of shame in his eyes. He needed to say so much: that from the humiliating scene his real self had been absent; that he was braver than they guessed; that he had great dreams for her, hope –

"Oh Elizabeth, I love you dearly!" he blurted. To his amazement he found she was in his arms, that this tall, beloved figure was pressed to his, that he was fervently kissing her neck. He drew his head back to look into her eyes.

They burned with the same excitement as his. The whole tigerish rectangle of her face was new, transformed. He was laughing, running a hand through her amazing hair.

"Why?" he asked. "Why, why, Elizabeth, why?"

"Seeing you facing them, I suddenly realized a glimpse of your whole life, its loneliness, its integrity – oh, Gary!"

They were laughing until he kissed that soft, predatory mouth. For months he had been separated from her, when her work had taken her to a Levantine sub-commission. He knew she had seen more of Lardening than of him recently. Yet always that peculiar sympathy had existed between them, making the time they were apart of little account.

His love and gratitude rose like a mist. She alone here knew the double game he constantly played.

VIII

Evening came again to the City, the lower angstrom output lowering the tensions generated during that day. Outside the City, true evening was still several hours away. On the Varne

Heights, where men and those like men fought and died, the sun shone, laying a thin and useless compress on the wounds that bled there. The City kept its own time, was its own world, marked its own crisis. For most of its oppressed terrestial inhabitants, it might have been a spaceship adrift in intragalactic night, so slight was their contact with their native Earth.

Yet change exists even in the most unchanged environment. The City itself was not the old City, only a smaller and newer version of it. For the terrestials who lived there, this change was minute, yet it was detectable, and made some indefinable difference in their lives.

And there was a more evident change. A section of open ground lay at one end of the native quarter of the City. Here Par-Chavorlem, playing the enlightened despot, had caused some sort of a fair to be erected for the duration of Synvoret's visit.

As a fair it was poor enough. A nul had his own ideas of entertainment, and did not indulge them in public as most biped races were accustomed to. Moreover, many of the attractions had not been adapted to the physical and mental capabilities of a subject race. There was a type of cinema, for instance, showing films only capable of resolution by a three-eyed species like nuls.

For all this, the fair had a certain kind of success among the sensation-starved terrestials of the City. At least the cafés scattered here and there about the grounds were well patronized.

Gary Towler sat contentedly enough at one of the tables, sipping a mild stimulant. He had arranged to meet Elizabeth here, and already his mood was lighter than it had been for some while.

For the first time, he saw the City-dwellers in something like a festive mood. Out in the crumbling Earth cities, some of the old local cultures still survived. Here in this alien race, they had long ago died. Yet it was possible, sitting here under an awning waiting for an attractive woman, to believe that *joie de vivre* might spring up again. A few couples were attempting self-consciously to dance to canned Partussian pop music.

He realized it was time Elizabeth arrived. Leaving the café, he began to move among the amusements. Of a sudden he caught sight of Elizabeth across the park. She was walking rapidly, with Chettle on one side of her, Wedman on the other. A stab of jealousy caught at Towler as he noticed the two interpreters. Hastily he began to follow, the jealousy yielding to a premonition of trouble.

The three figures moved ahead of him through the thin crowd. When Towler was nearly up to them, they disappeared into a round building. A drab grey, the round building announced itself as a place of entertainment only by the neon sign saying JARMBOREE over its entrance.

Indecisively, Towler stopped. He had no wish to intrude. Ordinarily he might have turned away, but today a sense of crisis was upon him. Fishing out a three-*byaksis* piece, he thrust it into the robot doorman, the door slid back, and he pushed forward into the building.

Inside, the circular chamber was dimly lit. The cacophonous funeral waltz thumped oppressively at his eardrums. Some hundred seats, large ones, built for nuls, were ranged round a central machine. Each seat was equipped with a kind of adjustable headpiece. This might have been a secret courtroom or even an operating theatre. Certainly it hardly looked like a place of entertainment. It was deserted except for Elizabeth and the two police interpreters.

"Gary!" Elizabeth called, with a note of unmistakable relief as she saw him enter. She started to come to him, but Chettle caught her by a slender waist.

"Stay here," he ordered. "Towler, what do you want?"

"I want Miss Fallodon."

"We're talking to her. Clear off."

"No, wait a minute!" Wedman said. He approached Towler casually. "Perhaps you'd better stay here. What we've got to say does concern you indirectly."

"All I need —" Towler began. That was as far as he got. Unexpectedly, Wedman had flung himself forward and delivered a terrific blow at Towler's solar plexus. The interpreter doubled up and fell, groaning.

Elizabeth cried out. Chettle also was disconcerted. He had imagined till now that Wedman was the man who took the orders.

"What did you do that for?" he asked. "It wasn't necessary."

"It's obvious, isn't it? Better to have Towler where we can keep an eye on him. We don't know whose side he's on.

Look at the way he followed us here. He's in Chav's pay most likely. The fewer risks we take the better. Come and give me a hand with him quickly. Elizabeth, you stay where you are. Towler's going to be quite safe."

Together, Chettle and Wedman half lifted, half dragged Towler into the nearest seat. The blow had stunned him. He offered no resistance.

"Better buckle him in here," Wedman said.

There were arm and leg clamps which snapped over him. Derisively, Wedman brought the headpiece down till it fitted over the back of Towler's head, over his temples, half around his throat.

"You'll do just fine there for a while," he said in a whisper. Then he surveyed the auditorium.

Just inside the entrance was a small control cubicle. Moving rapidly, Wedman went over to it and fiddled with switches. As he pressed one, the lights went off. Flicking them on again, he tried the next switch and the next. The entrance door slid tight.

"Good. Now we'll not be disturbed again," he said grimly, coming back to Chettle and the girl.

"Let me deal with Elizabeth," Chettle said in a quiet voice. The byplay with Towler had made him more uneasy than before.

"Go ahead. You know I like them plumper."

Chettle caught sight of Elizabeth's face, cold and still, only her eyes betraying her anger. He knew they had begun the wrong way to win her co-operation. In an unexpectedly gentle voice he said, "Elizabeth, I'm sorry about all this, really sorry. We're not a couple of thugs, but now there's a crisis on. Wedman's the nervous kind. Gary Towler's not hurt badly. We're not doing this for our sakes but for everyone's."

"The end as usual justifying the means," she said coolly. "All right, Cy, what do you want of me now that you have me locked in here?"

"We want you to kill Par-Chavorlem tonight," Wedman broke in harshly.

The nature of consciousness had changed, turning itself inside out to observe only the reverberating pain messages which, liberating themselves from Towler's stomach, plunged all over his system like startled fish. Long before those messages ceased, another signal came, demanding attention, growing to dominance.

This signal told Towler he was a nul. Gradually he became, through his human pain, more and more aware that he was inhuman. He was ten feet high, he was cylindrical. He moved slowly across a vast room in which two other nuls stood, their arms interlocking. Now they took hold of him, bending him backwards in a way grotesque yet delightful. Their eye-stalks interlocked. Encouraged, he was laying a sort of egg, a slippery, black-streaked ball of thick jelly which the other two nuls took up. The slippery ball was passed under one arm, then under another, moved with a curious dexterity, as if it was itself alive.

A horror like a toothache gnawed Towler. Sluggishly, he opened one eye. He was still a nul, but now through the shapes of his two companions he saw three bipeds talking together. One was a female. With a terrible effort of mind, he recognized her as someone he loved. Even the name came back. Elizabeth.

At that the hallucination in his mind slightly slipped. Now he seemed to be both nul and human. Trying to clear his vision, he shook his head. Wedman had fitted the headpiece without care. Now it loosened a little.

He became more aware of himself, of his surroundings. Still he was partly a nul, executing now a strange kind of natal dance – but he also realized he was undergoing a "Jarmboree." In this circular building, a mechanical adaptation of the principles of *jarm* trance had been applied commercially. The headpiece was inducing thoughts of a supposedly pleasant nature. Presumably if Towler had been a nul they would have been very pleasant.

Feebly, Towler tried to clear his head of the thundering images, but as long as he was clamped in the seat, the performance would go on. Now his arms were tightly interlocked with the other two nuls; they bore the egg between them, warm against their cylindrical bodies – yet at the same time he could hear something of what the three humans were saying.

"What is more, we can guarantee to get you safely away afterwards, right off the planet," one of them was saying. "The freighter *Geboraa* which brought Synvoret leaves for Saturn tomorrow. The oxygen-breathers among its crew have shore leave here in the City tonight. Wedman and I have spoken to one of them who guarantees he can get you aboard unseen and hide you in an empty fresh water tank."

"I can't do it, Cy," the girl called Elizabeth replied. Hers was the ideal beauty, hers the legs of a gazelle. "Attempts have been made on Chav's life before, all of them totally unsuccessful. A nul's a hard thing to kill. I'm not strong enough. Their hides are almost bulletproof, their flesh too solid."

"We've got a foolproof scheme," the other of the two men said impatiently. "You are interpreter on night duty in Chav's office tonight. Provoke him into taking hold of you."

They danced now intertwined, each with one arm extended, round and round giddily, the egg as a pivot between them. Their legs gouged into the earth, raining up dust, wrapping them in obscurity. The noise they made reverberated in every corridor of their being.

"You know his curious streak about women. We'll give you a knife. We've got it here. When he raises you in his arms, strike under them. That's where his vital spot is, under his arms."

"I can't do it."

"We'll be on hand if anything goes wrong."

"I can't do it."

They were not tired. They were inspired. Now the egg was the centre of the reeling universe. And the universe was triple. All came in threes, all order, all abandon. Three gods, three bodies, three points to the compass.

"You can't expect me to do it, it's crazy!"

"We must. It's a lot to ask but it's the only way."

"It's a fool's way, Cy. This has all been argued before, any number of times. If Chav were even hurt, Terekomy would have every one of us in the City killed."

"Maybe. But with Synvoret here his hands will be tied."

"Nonsense! He'd kill Synvoret too and blame us for his death."

"No more arguing, Elizabeth. We've got to try this. It's a chance but we've got to try it. See your dopey-looking boy friend there? Either you agree to try tonight or I cut his throat."

"I can't! You're crazy! Cy, don't let him. . . ."

"Towler'd be no loss."

"Don't, please!"

"Co-operate then, for God's sake!"

"Watch me. . . ."

Through the fertility dance he saw them approach. But even the three were now one, the ultimate. They whirled, blind to the universe, twisted in a crater of their own making, boring with the sharp flanges of their legs into the ground from which they had come. And now their arms lifted high above their heads, lips touching, and no more secrets, no more secrets. . . .

Even the heavy knife sharpened into a dagger which pressed against his throat meant nothing against the terrible union of that dance.

Even Elizabeth's painful cry did not fully pierce his trance.

Nothing could save him as Wedman leant forward – except the sudden bursting inward of the entrance door. Two of Terekomy's men stood there, lugging with them the fearsome Partussian version of a gun. They lunged forward with that graceless, seal-like walk.

Wedman's nerve went. Dropping the knife, he flung himself in a panic under the nearest seat, scrambling on hands and knees to escape. The gun exploded.

A square yard of the amphitheatre disintegrated. The *jarm* circuit was broken. Towler's mind was suddenly free of that erotic whirl, and the clamps on his arms and legs snapped up of their own accord. Wedman burst apart into glutinous morsels of flesh and marrow.

The police lumbered forward. Cy Chettle stood trembling where he was until they reached him. He offered no resistance as they led him away into a waiting three-wheeler. It drove off. Silence fell.

Gasping, Towler pulled himself to his feet. Quite apart from any pain he experienced, he felt emotionally drained. He made his legs move. Stiffly, he went over to Elizabeth and put an arm round her shoulder. She had not stirred since the police broke in. Her face was white, her full lips sucked in. When he touched her, it was as if a spell broke.

"You see, we're spied on all the time," she said in a whisper. "How did they know what was going on in here? How did they arrest the conspirators and let us go free?"

He laughed shakily, his courage coming back at the feel of her.

"Yet according to the labourers who helped erect these buildings, there was no wiring used but that required to work the actual device, the jarmboree. . . . By heavens, Elizabeth, I

64

have it! A delightful bit of Partussy cunning! In the head-pieces, an electrode induces impressions into the mind. It can receive outgoing impressions, too. In other words, it can see what's going on in my mind."

"It's a plausible guess," she said doubtfully.

"Darling, it's more than a guess. My blurred impressions of what Chettle and Wedman were saying to you must have been transmitted straight through to Police HQ here. Nice, eh? As soon as they saw there was a plot against Chav, they came and nabbed the conspirators, just in time."

Now she was more relaxed. She took his hand, stroking it, looking at him closely. Her searching look resolved into a smile.

"And you, the real plotter, got clean away!"

"Fortunately I was too muddled to think about friend Rivars. So with a fine gesture of contempt they leave us to our own devices!"

As he mentioned the name Rivars, his mind clouded. The mysterious piece of evidence had still not arrived from the leader. Mastering himself, he smiled and took her arm. Then the dagger that Wedman had threatened him with caught his eye. It lay gleaming dully in the aisle. Glancing guiltily round, he stooped, picked it up, and thrust it into his pocket. Then he took Elizabeth's arm again.

"It's still not late. Let's go and get a drink and something to eat at one of the new cafés. It'll do you good."

Sliding her hand into his, she walked beside him back into the Park. Now the place was almost deserted. The appearance of the police had evidently knocked the heart out of every-one's enjoyment. Indeed, Towler thought grimly, what cause for enjoyment was there? Tomorrow he would have to face Synvoret, the unknown quantity.

Despondently, as they turned into the nearest empty café, he set himself the task of being light-hearted.

They sat together in the café for an hour, talking or in com-panionable silence, until it was time for Elizabeth to go on night duty. By now their taut nerves had relaxed. Towler escorted her back to their official quarters before returning home. The place seemed as drab and empty as the inside of a box.

Only Peter Lardening was in the off-duty room as they entered, his shift of work over. Glancing up at them both with raised eyebrows, he said casually, "So! We hear you've had an eventful evening." He waved a hand at a notice still glittering wetly on the notice board.

Towler and Elizabeth went to read it. It announced simply that under the Colonial Conspiracies Act, Interpreter Wedman had been executed and Interpreter Chettle would be executed tomorrow for their involvement in a plot to murder high nuñ officials.

"Well?" Towler said interrogatively, turning to Lardening. He disliked the expression on the younger man's face.

"Rumour has it that the police came to *rescue* you from Chettle and Wedman, that you summoned them."

"Rumour's wrong, Lardening. Do you think Chav cares which of us lives or dies?"

"In your case I do. People in the park witnessed most of the incident. Whatever you are playing at, Towler, tread very carefully, or somebody will see you're put quietly out of the way."

He looked at Elizabeth as he spoke and added, almost to himself, "And then who would look after this lovely creature. . . ."

IX

Morning came, but with it no word or sign from Rivars.

Since his visit to Rivars' hideout, Towler had deliberately avoided all his underground contacts, lest either he or they were under suspicion. They would get in touch with him when they needed to.

He prayed that the evidence would soon arrive. It would jolt him into making up his mind as to what he should do. Until then, he could only carry on, playing the part that Rivars had instructed him to play, wondering ceaselessly if Par-Chavorlem's offer could be trusted. Towler had no way of knowing that before the day was out a third offer would be made to him.

Whatever Rivars was doing, he was not idle. His troops, after a stiff engagement with the Starjjan force, had driven them back into the broken territory of the Varne Heights. All the while, Terekomy's forces were holding a line to keep the combat from swinging towards the not so distant City. Yet Rivars had foxed them. Leading a small mounted guerilla column himself, he had slipped through the Partussian lines and devastated the small oil town of Ashkar, from which much of the City's oil was drawn.

Ashkar, unprotected by force screens, suffered casualties; nul and human. The blow to nul self-confidence and esteem was well-planned. Before the opposition could find him, Rivars' column was away again, fading into the night and the forest.

When Towler, primed by Terekomy and looking meeker than he felt, was brought before Synvoret and his retinue, the Signatory was preoccupied with the details of the Ashkar raid.

"You come of a bellicose species," were his first words to Towler.

"Yet we are not conquerors. We desire only peace, sir."

"Then why don't you accept the peace Partussy offers you?"

Towler fell silent. For as long as was necessary he must act like a contented colonial. Par-Chavorlem would know of it if he did not — his officers loitered here now in this small council chamber — and he would be whipped away, unable to help anyone, even himself. His job must be to propitiate the Signatory as far as possible until the moment came to drop all pretences, reveal the incontrovertible evidence, and cast himself upon Synvoret's mercy.

Synvoret's hide, at least where it was not covered by his uniform, was a milky grey patterned with fine wrinkles. He loomed above Towler, adding his silence to the interpreter's until at last he spoke.

"By doing such things as destroying oil wells you spoil your own material heritage. How does this affect you personally?"

"How can I be responsible for such an act?"

"That is far from being an answer, Interpreter, and I hope you have wits enough to know it. Now let me ask you another question. Suppose you and I are as dissimilar inwardly as we are outwardly. For what reason then, when I am back on Partussy, should we not send each other letters?"

This baffled Towler, not knowing what order of answer was expected of him. On impulse, he answered with a faint smile. "Because there is no correspondence between us."

The old nul raised an arm slightly, his comb rippling.

"Not only does that show me your excellent command of our language, Interpreter Towler. It shows there is some kind of correspondence between us, if you terrestials are capable of joking. Or perhaps it is an ability you caught from us."

It was Towler's turn to be silent, furious at this patronage, however pleased he was to find he had evidently passed some form of test. Synvoret patted him clumsily on the back, causing Towler to bump his forehead on the glass of his air helmet. As if this was a signal, Roifullery stepped forward.

"You can hold yourself in readiness to come with us out of the City, Interpreter," he said. "The Commissioner had arranged a full scale inspection of the City for us today, but we have postponed it because of this attack on Ashkar. The Signatory and I wish to go out overland to see for ourselves what is happening there. You will accompany us. The Commissioner will also be in the party."

This outing was not to Par-Chavorlem's taste. He had no mind to risk his own neck, nor was he keen to have the death of his distinguished visitor on his hands. That would look very suspicious far away on Partussy. Since Synvoret's request could not be refused outright, Par-Chavorlem laid every possible obstruction in the other's way, and it was not till midday that the small contingent moved off.

In one armoured car rode Synvoret, Par-Chavorlem and Towler. In another were Terekomy, Raggball and Roifullery. Escorting them came two high-powered meuron defence trucks, the next best thing to the impenetrable force screens, which could not be raised without heavy and elaborate equipment. They bowled smartly along one of the beautiful roads until reaching a certain checkpoint. Here they halted while the screens were damped, allowing them to drive through on to an unprotected and inferior paved way through chalky country.

For Towler, while the aliens sat in clumsy air suits, it was an absolute joy to breathe the cold breeze. The very meaning of life seemed to inhabit each lungful of air he took. This vital stuff Elizabeth should be breathing too.

"How long is it since you were outside the Commission City?" Synvoret inquired, turning to him.

"Ten years, sir."

"Why aren't you allowed to leave?"

"I am allowed it but refuse it. I have no connections outside the City." That was cunning, Towler thought. One lie for Chav, one lie for himself. "My parents, of the village of London, died long ago."

"You have friends inside the City?"

"Naturally I have, sir."

"Are you a lonely man, Interpreter?"

"All men are lonely, sir."

"Does not your habit of answering uninformatively make you more lonely than most men?"

No answer from Towler.

Par-Chavorlem's delaying tactics in the morning had allowed Terekomy time to stage the events of the afternoon.

Neither nul had any intention of letting the investigation team get near the real Ashkar. Their chief consideration here was discretion. A powerful nul family had purchased the Ashkar oil concession and settled on the spot. During Rivars' night raid, this family had been decimated, leaving two senior members to roar against Par-Chavorlem's folly. The truth was that indirectly they were as much victims of his oppression as the bipeds themselves, for all the financial advantages accruing.

These nuls could have complained direct to Synvoret in his own language, nor would Par-Chavorlem have been able to stop them telling the truth. Therefore Synvoret could only be allowed to believe he had been to Ashkar. Accordingly, a fake Ashkar was established in an area of perfect safety that had been cleared of Rivars' forces. The native labour which had been wounded at Ashkar was transported here to lend realism to the scene. Fires were started. Other people were brought from the City to increase the confusion. Partussian soldiery in operational kit moved about in businesslike fashion, occasionally discharging annihilators at an imaginary enemy.

The armoured cars drew up, sheltered by a fern-covered bank.

"I don't think we'd better go any further, Signatory," Par-Chavorlem said. "We are only a few hundred yards from the firing line."

The party climbed down, standing in the road rather helplessly without speaking. Two miles away, beyond foreground cover, stood a line of wooded hills, their very silence seeming an indication of the presence of enemy forces. An ambulance sped hurriedly by, flying only two feet above the ground and making for Commission hospital. A burly nul officer came up, bowed smartly, and consulted with Terekomy in a monotone.

Synvoret and Roifullery stood sniffing the air like old war

horses. The excitement of battle played its little drum in their veins, making them feel young and restless.

With a whiff of freedom in his nostrils, Towler too was restless. Rivars could not be so far away. Yet there was no way of contacting him. Nor would the patriot leader know he was here, away from the City.

To complete Par-Chavorlem's spurious picture, a slow stream of terrestial refugees, brought specially to the spot from the Commission for this performance, straggled past the two stationary vehicles, clutching bundles or humping sacks. Towler, as ignorant as the Signatory about what was really happening, felt his heart go out to these people.

"The attackers came through the woods behind us," Terekomy announced, "thus taking Ashkar from its least defendable side. As you heard in the briefing yesterday, the civil war had not spread this far – until last night. Obviously both sides are interested in the oil. We export most of it. They would put it to military use."

"Why was not your Arm in greater strength at such a strategic point?" Synvoret asked.

The Arm Marshall rippled his comb.

"Colonial regulations allow me only five hundred nuls for the planet, sir. It is too little. But we must abide by the regulations."

Towler felt a strong urge to vomit.

A tired group of refugees were moving past them. Gazer Roifullery pointed with his cane to an old woman staggering by with a suitcase, her face stained by sweat and dirt.

"Ask that one where she is making for," he said to Towler.

Halting the old woman gently, Towler translated the question for her. She listened, her eyes still fixed anxiously down the road before she turned to him. The look she gave him, although full of hopelessness, had nevertheless a little core of personal anger in it for him, a fraternizer with the aliens. It jarred Towler as if, biting into a soft fruit, he had split a tooth on the stone.

"They took me from the Commission. Now I'll have to make my way back to the Commission on foot," she said. "And I'm not getting a *byaksis* for doing it."

Not entirely understanding this answer, Towler still had the presence of mind to give it the required propaganda slant when translating it to the Psycho-Watch nul.

"She says she is making for the safety of the Commission."

"Ask her what has happened at her home," Roifullery ordered.

The old woman stood there mulling over the question when it was repeated to her, disregarding the other refugees brushing past her.

"Tell the ugly bastard I don't know what he's talking about. He must know more about this stunt than I do. I don't know a thing."

"The old lady is dazed. She does not seem to understand you."

"Ask her if her home has been destroyed. She must understand that."

"I don't know what is happening here," Towler said to her. "You must try to help me. Was your home destroyed in last night's attack?"

"I've got one room in Commission City, which is okay. I was brought out here this morning and now I'm getting back. As to what's happening here, I tell you I know nothing. Any more silly questions?"

Glancing at Par-Chavorlem's comb, Towler saw a certain tension there, the Commissioner regretting not having briefed Towler thoroughly on the situation beforehand. Hesitating, playing for safety, Towler said to Roifullery, "She says that Rivars' men destroyed her house early this morning."

"Ask her where the rest of her family is."

"Where is the rest of your family?"

"Oh, go to the devil," said the old lady, moving off.

"She says, all dead, sir," Towler reported.

His hesitancy had lent the little incident a weight it would not otherwise have had. Synvoret had listened with absolute interest. He now came forward, speaking in a low voice to Par-Chavorlem.

"Just how reliable is this interpreter, Commissioner? He seems to me to be holding something back. I would like you personally to interrogate one of these refugees. Ask them if they think we are taking stern enough measures against the rebels."

A moment of difficulty had slipped into something far worse.

Par-Chavorlem drew himself up stiffly.

"I have every faith in my interpreter," he said. "Some of

71

these natives speak a villainous dialect, which no doubt made his task a little difficult. . . ."

"Nevertheless. I would like you to interrogate one of these creatures," insisted Synvoret. "Try this fat creature approaching with the little one on its back."

This time there could be no evasion.

"I do not personally speak their barbaric tongue," Par-Chavorlem said with dignity. "They have many different dialects over the globe, all of them illogical."

Synvoret turned around and appeared to be minutely examining a bush. At last he spoke in a low voice.

"Commissioner, does it not seem to you that for some understanding of the native's habits, his laws, his customs, his religion, his ceremonies, his philosophy, his literature, his history; for some understanding of all or any of these vital things, does it not seem necessary to you to have a knowledge of his language?"

"You are assuming, Signatory, sir, that an understanding of these things helps a governor to govern. On this wretched planet it is not so."

Synvoret's comb was flushed and angry.

"What you say is tantamount to an admission that you govern without understanding," he said quietly.

"Very far from it. Justice is one thing – whomever it is applied to. That assumption is the very basis of our legal and administrative systems."

A tremendous explosion to one side of them broke the tension. Earth, stones, and clods scattered high, showering the party. The whole group of Partussians dropped clumsily to the ground for protection, floundering in their air suits. After a minute of silence, they raised their heads. Another explosion sent them prone again.

"The enemy are counter-attacking," Par-Chavorlem said. "That requires very little understanding. It is my duty, Signatory, to see you back to safety. If you please, we will leave now and return to the City as expediently as possible."

In that moment, Towler saw clearly that this whole manoeuvre was a deception. He could identify the noise of the explosion as a stereosonic one. The patriots did not possess these latest field weapons – which Synvoret would never have heard in action. The two explosions were therefore a diversion staged by Par-Chavorlem's own side, impressive but harmless.

Towler recalled that Terekomy had quietly left their party a moment ago. The Arm Marshall had saved a trying situation with an impromptu bang.

Angrily, Towler remembered what the old refugee woman had said, and now her meaning was clear. Wherever they were, they were not near Ashkar. Whatever the truth was, Synvoret would not find it here. Towler himself did not know what was happening.

Now he was alarmed. Par-Chavorlem's plans, started two years ago, were maturing. Unless a spoke was put in them, they would succeed.

As they bundled back into the vehicles without too much dignity, Terekomy returned, solid, slow, every inch a soldier.

"There's no danger, gentlemen," he said. "It just happens that we are within range of the rebel guns. If we withdraw rapidly up the next side we might be in time to see our counter-measures."

They lurched forward. The side road climbed a hill. When Terekomy announced that they were out of the imaginary danger, the party halted and looked back across the quiet countryside.

"Ah, the counter-measures!" Par-Chavorlem exclaimed, pointing ahead.

Over the line of wooded hills to their front played a momentary strange light. Valleys, streams, silent woods, all were picked out clearly for a second before vanishing entirely. Steaming red earth sagged and gasped like a broken mouth where no patriot had been. Ten square miles of country had been sacrificed to the Commissioner's little charade.

"Ah, give 'em a bit of their own medicine!" Gazer Roifullery exclaimed. His comb had turned very pallid. Towler also was pale.

Terekomy's five hundred toughs were more than ample. Fifty of them could reduce all Earth to red ruin in a week, given this encouragement. He was both impressed and shattered by this show of force.

So evidently were Synvoret and Roifullery. They rode back to the City in rapt silence.

X

They were back in the impenetrable security of the City, and here, Towler felt, was the greatest danger to himself. He now had no man he could call a friend. After the execution of Chettle this morning, he had been ostracized. Elizabeth was the only one who would defy the ban and still talk to him.

He wanted to go to her. He was on duty and could not go. Bored, he sat at the back of a small conference room while Synvoret indulged in a post mortem on his recent excursion. Towler hardly bothered to listen to his argument. Since the Signatory had been provided with false premises, how could it matter what conclusion he came to?

In a while, however, a more ponderous note in Synvoret's voice made him sit up. The Signatory was rebuking the Commissioner.

". . . I cannot help feeling you were ill-advised to let this civil war break out at all," he was saying.

"According to charter, we let these bipeds govern themselves as far as possible," Par-Chavorlem replied. "They are primitive by nature and pugnacious by disposition. If they elect to fight each other, then it is unwise to forbid them, or the wave of bad feeling turns against us. You must know how difficult it is to deal with a planetary uprising. For one thing, reinforcements from other Vermilion sector planets will always take too long to get here. So we prefer to let our terrestial squabblers get on with it, containing the conflict by limiting their arms and movements. Ours must always be the gently guided hand."

It was a smooth answer. Of the truth, that Earth was in actual fact united in hatred of Partussy and Par-Chavorlem, none of the nuls present could catch a glimpse.

Gazer Roifullery said, "Though I think you should press Castacorze for more reinforcements now, in the main you are well advised to rule so liberally. Earth was once a frontier planet; it is no longer. I agree that full-scale rebellions on anything but frontier planets are surprisingly difficult to put down."

"What's that?" Terekomy demanded sharply. He had

never had trouble in stamping down any show of insurrection. "Why the distinction between frontier and colonial planets?"

"We have studied the problem carefully at Psycho-Watch," Roifullery answered. "Imagine the expanding sphere of Partussian influence as a balloon being blown up, space routes rather than air pressure causing its expansion. The balloon's surface represents our perimeter of conquest, the frontier planets. It is here we have to place the greatest concentration of our forces, as you know, Arm Marshall. Once a new planet comes inside the perimeter – in other words when it is subdued – a Commission is set up, and the main body of forces have to press ever on."

"Obviously enough, but –"

"The balloon analogy will also show you," Roifullery continued, ignoring Terekomy's interruption, "that the larger the Empire grows, the more thinly its forces are spread. As time goes by, we are less and less able to spare nuls and weapons from the perimeter areas to cope with trouble far behind their lines. Too much pressure on the frontier and the whole balloon collapses. That is why, recently, some rebel planets have been allowed to triumph and retain their independence. Only a comparatively weak blow is needed to knock them flat again. But that weak blow is often not worth the expense. In future we must hold what we have. This is a lesson you should remember."

When at last Towler was freed for the evening, he sought out Elizabeth in a whirl of excitement. He took her into his arms, pulling her up, folding his arms around her, pressing her to him.

"You should have heard what Roifullery let slip, darling! Perhaps he had forgotten I was there, or perhaps after the poor show I gave outside this afternoon he thought I wouldn't understand. We are trying now merely to boot out Par-Chavorlem and get a just Commissioner in his place. But from what Roifullery says it seems that if we could only overthrow the nuls, the Empire would make no further effort to reclaim us. Earth just isn't that important."

"I can hardly believe it. They're too grasping to abandon anything."

"That's what he said. Here under Chav with a rigid censorship it's impossible to know how the Empire actually fares. It must be more vulnerable than we believed. Oh, Elizabeth, if only we –"

He stopped.

"What are you smiling at?" he asked.

"This mood suits you," she said. "I've never seen you more animated. Darling, take care of yourself. Don't go looking for trouble!"

"I care nothing for myself, Elizabeth, everything for you. Earth means nothing to me, you are everything. I'd do anything to see you free and happy, anything!"

They kissed, suddenly and ravenously, as if their lives depended on it.

"Ah, Gary dear, how curious the different view of you I've had in the last few days," she said at last, running a hand gently over his hair. "The breath of fresh Earth air has done you good.... You know when I first was brought here two years ago I thought of you all as captives. I suppose I despised you. Now I see that you at least have so much more to you."

"I told you. I've a tiger inside, even when I mew like a kitten," he said half-jokingly, drawing her down into a chair.

"Then I hope you were right when you said I have one in me too. You see ... I've not ... I've never been fully roused, Gary. Oh Gary...."

Again, as his hand cupped her breasts, she kissed him. His senses rose up like smoke.

After a few minutes, he said to her, "Elizabeth, my love, let me speak to you in Partussian."

"Whatever for?"

"Curiosity really. You know how I feel about them, yet for me it's a pleasure to speak their tongue." Without a pause, he switched into that language. And at once it seemed as if his understanding of things altered, as if his perceptions as well as his words were translated to another plane. "It's such an ancient tongue, Elizabeth. After a while, you seem to feel its hoariness. Remember, it was established in its present form almost before there were true men on Earth. It's hard to credit, isn't it? To me, it has become almost a physical force. It has helped form me nearly as much as my environment has."

"I don't wish to use it to you," Elizabeth said, speaking in Partussian nevertheless. "It has none of the softness in it I wish for you. Talking it, I understand why the nuls have no poets."

76

"Yes, it fits their nature, inflexible and without ardour. Yet undoubtedly this language has been a factor in their universal success in conquest. It's a language for soldiers, for rulers, for administrators."

He broke off, laughed, and added in English, "But not a language for lovers, as you say. And at present I hardly want to talk at all. I'm mad, Elizabeth, mad. I could walk straight into Synvoret now and tell him everything!"

"You must be careful, Gary. Whatever happens, things have got to go on as they are until you hear from Rivars. He's the leader."

Towler pulled an impatient face.

"He's as fallible as the rest of us."

"That's not true. He wouldn't be leader if he was. We must wait until he sends the evidence for Synvoret."

But the evidence did not come, and so another vital day of Synvoret's visit passed.

Next morning, Towler was at the palace early. As he entered the alien personnel wing, the daily four-truck convoy was just leaving for the original City. It reminded Towler that without doubt Par-Chavorlem would have everyone back there within a fortnight, with many of their present potentials for freedom lost.

Nobody spoke to him. Passing Peter Lardening in the corridor, Towler thought he detected a slight nod, but all the other interpreters studiously ignored him.

All right, you curs, he told himself, you'll see ... Yet he had to admit that what they would see he did not know. If he could find out how thoroughly Synvoret was being taken in by Par-Chavorlem's bluff he felt it might help.

On this point at least, light was soon shed.

Half the morning was spent idling about behind Synvoret, his secretary, his bodyguard and Roifullery. They were inspecting the Treasury. Roifullery, aided by the secretary, was going thoroughly through the records. Synvoret addressed a few questions via Towler to the terrestial assistants present, but made no attempt to conceal his boredom. When at last they were finished, Synvoret made off smartly for his suite in the palace.

"I want you to follow me, Interpreter," he said.

Towler did as he was told, trotting behind the four vast

figures of the Partussians. He thought, as he so often had thought in moments of impotent fury during the last ten years, "If a Partussian physically attacked me, I should be helpless, even with a knife." A knife was the only weapon he had; he still nursed beneath his tunic the weapon with which Wedman had tried to kill him in the Jarmboree.

Once in the signatorial suite, the aliens removed their air suits.

Towler stood stiff and wary in the middle of the room while the nuls relaxed. After ten years of forced mixing with them, it could hardly be said that he found them strange. Yet as they sank into chairs, he felt a wonder at the flipperiness of their arms and legs and at the cylindrical immensity of their bodies. Gently but firmly, Synvoret shooed his secretary and body-guard out of the room before turning to Towler.

"Now then, Interpreter Towler," began Synvoret genially, "you and I must get to know each other a little better. My visit to Earth is only a brief one – I have only five more whole days left – but there is every reason why in that time we should be friends. Why don't you come and sit down?"

"Thank you, sir, the chairs do not fit me – or I do not fit the chairs. I prefer to stand."

"As you wish. You see, Interpreter, very much depends upon the sort of understanding you and I reach. One might almost be dramatic and say that the future of Earth depends on it."

When Towler did not respond, he made an impatient movement with his comb.

"I do wish you'd sit down and make yourself as comfortable as possible, Interpreter. You understand that what I am going to say is quite unofficial and need not be repeated outside these walls. Do you recall the name of Wattol Forlie? He was a nul who held the post of Third Secretary to the Commissioner until two years ago."

"No," Towler said. "My work rarely brings me into contact with anyone but the First Secretary."

"No matter. I came here to make an investigation into terrestial affairs. I wished for unescorted travel anywhere I desired but the Commissioner thinks that owing to the present somewhat dangerous situation this is not advisable. Obviously, this curtails my freedom to inquire. My schedule for the next five days is full. Nevertheless, it will hardly allow the opportunities for free observation that I required. You understand what I am saying?"

"Indeed yes." It was both obvious and encouraging. Synvoret had not swallowed Par-Chavorlem's bait yet. He was still thinking independently.

"You may not understand as well as you think you do," Roifullery broke in severely. He moved restlessly, curling a leg. "All the Signatory is saying is that naturally enough the Commissioner wishes to show us the most favourable side of his establishment. We require a neutral view – again, naturally enough."

Danger signs flashed between the two nuls.

"I am here to look for trouble," Synvoret said. "For Trinity's sake, sit down, Interpreter."

"I would prefer to stand, sir, thank you."

"Don't mistake me. All I wish to do is confirm that everything on Earth is as well-run as it appears to be."

At this Roifullery's comb relaxed, but Synvoret continued.

"Some small points here and there, however, confuse the general scheme. You, for instance, speak our language very competently. Why were you so hesitant with the refugee woman at Ashkar yesterday morning? Were you translating accurately what she said?"

"Yes, sir. I was somewhat scared, sir, knowing we were in an exposed position." Oh God, how long would he have to lie! Neither his friend Rivars nor his enemy Par-Chavorlem knew what they were demanding of him.

Synvoret smoothed his comb and said, "I am not a fool, Interpreter. Having served in colonies myself, I am aware of the pressures you may be under. Let me put the situation to you in a nutshell. I am a plenipotentiary with the full backing of the Colony Worlds Council, which has sent me here to investigate a charge of corruption and, in particular, exploitation."

"It might be wiser, sir –" Roifullery began, getting up, but Synvoret ignored him entirely.

"Let me say at once, that a certain amount of exploitation is inevitable in any senior-junior relationship. With petty instances of this I am not concerned. What does concern me is how true may be some information I have that the Commissioner is virtually a dictator here, trampling over you terrestials. Since you are the terrestial with whom I had closest contact, I naturally question you on the point. You need have no fear about answering me as your conscience sees fit."

Towler maintained silence.

Synvoret's and Roifullery's eye-stalks swivelled towards one another. The latter said something that Towler did not catch. Synvoret nodded.

"Wait here a moment, Interpreter," he said.

He and Roifullery lumbered into the next room, leaving Towler standing uncomfortably in his air suit. One part of his mind registered the fact that these two nuls were obviously not in complete accord. Mainly he was full of worry; the fantastic idea seized him that they might torture him into speaking, that they had gone to fetch their tough Raggball for that purpose.

Nobody could be trusted: he was not even sure of himself.

The nuls were away for two minutes. Evidently they had reached some sort of agreement. Roifullery spoke.

"Obviously it is in your own interest and in the interest of your species to be perfectly truthful with us. If your Commissioner is a just man, then you must say so to retain him here. If he is unjust, then you must say so to us, that he may be removed."

Again the ghastly sulphuric silence, in which Towler told himself that even these beings, seemingly honest though they were, were only Partussians, and therefore as untrustworthy as Par-Chavorlem himself. Unlikely though it seemed in view of what had been said, they might even have been converted to Par-Chavorlem's way of thinking, and were now testing his loyalty. His moment of truth must, *must* wait until the irrefutable evidence came from Rivars. Sweat burst out on his forehead, damping the inside of his helmet.

"We appreciate," Synvoret continued after a minute, "that your silence may have been bought with threats or promises. So we must assure you, before you commit yourself, that anything you may reveal to us will be secret, and that you can, if you wish, leave Earth in the *Geboraa* when we do to escape any possible retribution." Abruptly, Towler sat down on one of the vast chairs, he could guess what was coming next.

"To show how warmly I shall regard anything you may tell us in confidence, let me say this," continued the Signatory. "In my younger days, I was a Commissioner in this same Vermilion Sector of space. The planet Starjj was my responsioility. I still own by Imperial Charter one island on it, an island consisting of one-twentieth of the land surface, and stretching from temperate zone to equator. Starjj is an oxygen-nitrogen planet much like yours, its gravity's similar, its peoples peaceable, and bipedal like you. In return for your undivided co-operation with me here, I am prepared to take you, and any other terrestials you name up to one dozen, to the island of Starjj which I own. It will then be given to you and your heirs in perpetuity. You will be more than a free man. You will be a ruler in your own right. I have the power to do all this and more.

"I will tell you frankly that I am disappointed in finding you somewhat uncommunicative, but I realize you may have your reasons. Now you had better go away and think over what I have said. Tomorrow the Commissioner wishes me to accompany him on a hunting expedition, so I shall not need you. We will meet and talk here tomorrow night, when I hope you will have decided to give me your full co-operation. Leave us now."

Gary Towler left in a sort of daze. Rivars' offer, Par-Chavorlem's offer, now Synvoret's offer, each bigger than the last; they bewildered him, as the sudden sight of water bewilders a thirsty man in a desert, reaching down and soaking all the fibres in his being with their promise. Under the circumstances, the burden of deciding anything was so like a physical burden that he almost collapsed in the corridor outside the Signatory's suite.

None of the three promises were to be trusted – Rivars' perhaps least of all. For if Par-Chavorlem and all his surplus men were removed from Earth, in the uprising which would undoubtedly follow Rivars might well be swept away by rival leaders. And how much was Synvoret's word worth? He after all was only a nul....

Weakly, he made his way out of the palace and through the streets towards Elizabeth's apartment. He must talk this over with her; with her he could sort out his troubled mind, her wits were as deft as her long fingers.

Elizabeth too had been talking, equally without very comfortable results. As she came off afternoon shift, she waylaid Peter Lardening, who was emerging from Transmissions, and arranged to meet him ten minutes later in one of the small cafés of the native quarter.

He rose as she entered the alcove he had reserved. His manner was uneasy.

"It's good to get this chance to talk to you, Elizabeth. You seem to have been avoiding me lately."

"How odd. I notice people seem to be avoiding me."

"You must know why that is. For your own good, Elizabeth, I feel I must tell you –"

"Please, Peter! Remember I wanted to talk to you."

"All right. Go ahead. I've ordered cocoa. I'll drink it quietly and listen." He looked offendedly across at her, slowly relaxing. "You're a very unconventional girl, you know, Elizabeth."

Elizabeth dropped her eyes, struck by the memory of Towler's calling her conventional. By so much her image in two men's eyes differed. These last few days she had become self-conscious; aware of the way she behaved and spoke, aware of the movement of her narrow thighs when she walked.

"I want to talk to you about Gary Towler," she said. "He's been treated unfairly. It's childish to ostracize him. Peter, I want you to use your influence with the other interpreters to get this stupidity stopped."

"Not until he stops playing Chav's game." Lardening checked himself as the cocoa arrived. When the waiter had gone, he continued on a different tack.

"Look here, Elizabeth, it's probably obvious to you that I'm fond of you. So allow me to warn you. Towler's no good to you. He's no good to anyone at present. I used to admire him. Now I don't know what's happening in his mind. It's noticed that he comes to your apartment – everything's noticed in this damned hole. Take it from me, it doesn't do to associate with him. If you can't see why, never mind why. Just try and avoid him."

"Peter, Gary needs help, not suspicion." She was on the verge of telling him of Towler's connection with Rivars, but discretion got the better of her.

"This is a dangerous city, Elizabeth. There's nothing but suspicion here. We're all suspect. Terekomy's men were hunting down some poor guy as I came here. A crisis is brewing. Can't you *feel* it?"

He lit an aphrohale, sucking it in nervously and looking around the café as he did so.

"Tension's growing everywhere. We feel it, the nuls feel it.

Five days before Synvoret leaves.... And sometime during those five days, hell is going to break loose. I just don't want to see you involved in it. But Towler will be involved if he's not careful, and that's why I tell you to keep away from him."

Elizabeth drummed the slender fingers of one hand on the table.

"You can't scare me away from the man I love, you know," she said quietly.

For a long painful second he stared into her eyes. Then he rose.

"If you feel like that. . . ." he said.

He flung a coin at the waiter as he left. Elizabeth did not call him back. His cocoa was untouched.

She lifted her own cup thoughtfully to her lips. She saw the situation on Earth as perhaps nobody else did. The contest was not simply between Par-Chavorlem and the Signatory. It was a four-sided contest, formed by two nuls and two Earthmen: Chav, Synvoret, Rivars, and Gary. Not one of them trusted the other three. Gary, who held the weakest hand, was slowly being thrust into the most exposed position. Surely there was something else she could try to help him?

Suddenly she saw what it was. Putting down her cup, she too left the café.

* * * * *

Before going to Elizabeth's place, Towler took a long stroll to try and clear his mind first. It hurt him even as he walked to see how the other humans of the Commission now shunned him, how a shopkeeper's wife pulled her small son out of his path.

All along, since before his secret visit to Rivars, he had determined to do everything possible for the oppressed people of his planet. Yet he was not alone any more. He had Elizabeth to think of now. Given the chance, he might win her. For that, too, he would do everything possible.

Now he saw that these two objectives had miraculously ceased to conflict. If only Rivars produced that wretched piece of evidence before tomorrow night. Towler had merely to hand it to Synvoret. Synvoret would reward him with the island on Starjj; Par-Chavorlem would be on his way out. . . .

With a pang, he recalled his doubts of Rivars' capabilities.

83

Stifling them, he burst into a run. He could wait to see her no longer.

Elizabeth was not in her apartment.

"Elizabeth!" he called.

No answer. No note. No sign.

All his insecurities came crowding back on him in new guise. He trusted no one. Everyone was against him, and in consequence, against Elizabeth. And she was his future.

No terrestial quarters were allowed any sort of communication device with other quarters. He could not phone or radio, although the palace could summon him.

He left the block of apartments at a trot, hurrying back to the palace. She should not be there. Her brief afternoon's duty finished two hours before this. Still, he must look there for her. Seeing a nul police guard eye him from the opposite side of the street, Towler dropped into a walk.

Elizabeth was not at the palace. Only Meller and Johns were in the interpreter's room. They would not speak at first, until under pressure of his agitation they were forced to take notice. Then they too became alarmed. They had not seen her since she left to go off duty two hours ago.

It occurred to Towler that she had perhaps gone to his apartment. This was unlikely, for since Towler's banishment, they had agreed that in future it was better for her if they met at hers. All the same, perhaps. . . .

In an access of hope, he collected a new oxygen pack, fitted it, and set out once more. Silently, he called her name over and over to himself.

Supposing she had been arrested? There was never a dearth of trumped-up charges in the City. Supposing those vague rumours about Par-Chavorlem were true, and he had got her? Or supposing Rivars had her hostage, to ensure Towler's obedience? Were even the other interpreters to be trusted? Most of them hated him since the Wedman-Chettle affair. His thoughts grew wilder and more strained.

"Towler!"

Startled, he looked up. He was nearly home, half-running through the native quarter. The butcher had halted him.

"My delivery boy's behind today," he said. "If you're going home, could you take the meat you ordered with you? I've got it here."

84

"Give it to me then," Towler said impatiently. He had forgotten he had ordered any meat.

As soon as the butcher presented him with a parcel, he hurried on, pressing impatiently into the airlock of his block of apartments. Unclamping the face of his helmet, he sprinted down the corridor to his rooms and burst in.

No familiar graceful form awaited him. There was no note, nothing. Baffled, helpless, he stood where he was. Now no doubt existed in his mind that something horrible was closing in on him. He felt shakily for reassurance beneath his air suit. The knife was still there – if only he knew at whom to strike.

He hated, overflowing with it, as an animal stinks of hatred when it crouches in a trap.

His eyes fell on the butcher's package lying on the table where he had flung it. Suddenly he knew why the butcher had broken silence to speak to him. He had ordered no meat.

This was the evidence from Rivars!

Ironic that when it finally arrived he should feel so indifferent to the patriot leader and all his affairs. Nevertheless, he must make a move in some direction, if only to relieve his feeling of anguished impotence.

With a great effort, Towler picked up the package and took it into the kitchen.

"This had better be good," he said aloud. If it convinced Synvoret, perhaps he would help in the finding of Elizabeth.

He undid the paper. Inside was canvas and he unwrapped that.

His face fell in sudden dismay as he uncovered the contents. Puzzlement, anger, fear, followed the dismay. Although there was no accompanying note, clearly this could have come from nobody else but Rivars. But what did it mean? Had Rivars lost faith in him? Could it be some sort of a cruel joke? Above all, to whom had it belonged?

Clutching the table edge. Towler stared down in horror and despair. Amid the wrappings lay a bloody human foot, severed at the ankle.

XI

Gary Towler did not touch the foot. Shocked disappointment seized him. A dark tide of cascading pictures poured through his mind, so that he shut his eyes and grasped the table. Momentarily he seemed to be outside the enveloping pudding of the City, riding on a black mare through detaining bushes towards freedom. Or he was his own self, but translated into that peculiar self he felt himself to be when he was using the cold unmetaphorical tongue of Partussy. His blood recreated again the stamping of the nul mating dance as he had heard it in the Jarmboree.

Slowly this peculiar whirl of emotion left him. Weakly, he wondered at it. After all, this was only a message from Rivars, and why should Rivars mean so much to him?

Shocked disappointment was playing tricks in his mind.

He put the canvas back over the foot.

He went slowly into the living room, still wearing his air suit, and lay back in the solitary armchair. The whole situation needed to be reviewed and analysed. Yet before he made that mental effort he thought distastefully of life itself, the daily drip of consciousness on to the cold slab of memory. Though its taste was sweet, it washed down too many ghastly things.... Why need he face this voiceless, heavy foot, or all that it implied.

For it implied either that he had been betrayed by Rivars. Or that Rivars himself had been betrayed!

Suppose the former. Rivars, no longer willing to entrust Towler with the real evidence against Par-Chavorlem, sent him instead this gruesome token that relationships were severed between them.

Suppose the latter. Rivars had been betrayed by... well, the butcher seemed a likely guess. If the butcher had accepted a nul bribe, who but he would more likely to have a bloody foot at his disposal? And Towler by accepting the package from him had demonstrated his own complicity. If all this were so, it would not be long before Arm Marshall Terekomy's nuls were at Towler's door.

Perhaps they would simply shoot down the airlock, so that he died gasping his lungs out in their beastly air. Or more likely they would take him to one of those buildings innocent men never entered, where he would die more slowly.

He stood up.

He must act while there was the chance for action.

Clamping up his faceplate, Towler hurried down to the street. Clearly his immediate line of approach lay through the butcher. He had to discover whether the fellow was still his ally or his enemy.

The butcher was about to close, his shop was empty. He looked up startled as Towler came through the airlock.

"You should keep away," he said. He was wiping a chopper. "We never know when we're being watched. Nobody has better reason than you to keep that in mind."

"The parcel from Rivars. You know what was in it?"

The butcher looked curiously at Towler's pale face. He put down the chopper and came round from behind the counter.

"I had no business to look. That's entirely your affair. Besides, it had not been here for more than a few minutes when I saw you. The man who smuggled it into the City was delayed."

His expression was frightened. He did not look like a guilty man.

"What's the matter?" he asked, when Towler was silent. "What have you come here for?"

"Something's gone wrong."

"Not as far as I know."

"You'd better come to my apartment to see."

"I can't do that! God, don't you realize how suspicious it would look. I can't be seen with you. I don't want to get myself more implicated than I am! At this stage, we dare not risk —"

"You must come with me. Please, it's vital."

Both of them heard with surprise the note of pleading in Towler's voice. The butcher shrugged. Then he wiped his hands in his apron.

"Give me two minutes," he said.

He put up the shutters and closed the shop. Going into his rear room, he struggled into an air suit and let Towler out by the back door. Now Towler breathed more easily. In his own flat he could face this man. If it came to a crisis, he would have his own knife and the butcher would not have his. Yet by the very way the man complied with his wishes Towler was disarmed.

"What's the matter?" the butcher asked, as they entered Towler's block a moment later. "Don't you believe this package came from Rivars?"

"See for yourself," Towler said, leading the way into his kitchen.

There on the table the package still lay. The butcher

87

approached slowly, turning back the wrappings. The foot was revealed. Strands of black hair sprouted from the big toe.

Without comment, his face wooden, the butcher stared at it. Towler too looked more closely. The toes seemed abnormally long. Between them was some kind of greyish membrane. The butcher took hold of the foot, lifted it, spread out the toes. Between each of them ran strong membrane, linking them as the ribs of a fan are linked. When he released them, the toes slowly came together once more, the membrane folding up until it was scarcely visible.

"What is it?" Towler asked huskily, his mind swept blank.

"It's a Starjjan foot," the butcher said.

"Not a human foot!" Towler echoed, and at once the situation became clear to him, billowing out through the reaches of his understanding like a spinnaker.

This foot had belonged to a member of that web-footed race, a few thousand of whom Arm Marshall Terekomy had illegally smuggled on to Earth to fight Rivars. No doubt the bloody bit of evidence had been obtained in the morning's fighting, and had been passed along the underground to Towler as speedily as possible. Rivars had fulfilled his promise, certain this was indisputable proof that the present government exceeded its right. Placed in the right hands, it would remove Par-Chavorlem once and for all, for an infringement of the Partussian galactic law that one subject species was forbidden on the planet of another subject species was invariably dealt with harshly.

By good fortune, Synvoret had served on the planet Starjj. When shown the foot, he would recognize it for what it was. He could instigate a general inquiry, Earth would have justice done.

Towler thought momentarily of Rivars, who had after all planned well. Now the responsibility had passed from him to Towler.

"Funny the way you got into such a panic when you first saw this foot," the butcher observed. "You've endangered the whole operation, the way you carried on. I keep asking myself why you carried on like that, coming running to me."

He was a short thickset man with greasy grey hair, his gaze shortsighted but perceptive. At the moment his manner was more curious than reproving. He peered up at Towler, who moved uneasily.

"I thought Rivars had failed me," said Towler almost in a whisper.

"*Me* or *us* do you mean? Listen, I'm not in this stunt for the glory but for what I can make out of it. I'm not as ignorant as I look on the surface. What I chiefly go for is old books that I get smuggled in from the cities. That's my hobby, you could say. The old cities of Earth have still got books from the old days in them, you know. And so I study up about human beings and what goes on in their minds, and do you know what I think?"

Faintly embarrassed, Towler said he did not.

"I think that for some reason that you may not even know yourself, you *wanted* Rivars to fail."

"That's nonsense, absolute nonsense!" Towler said.

The butcher merely smiled.

"Well, you wouldn't examine this foot properly for yourself, would you? Something in your subconscious wanted me as a witness of what you took for Rivars' mistake."

"I needed your help."

"Ah, now you're rationalizing."

Suddenly Towler was furiously angry. He scorned and resented this blunt man's probing. Growling, he grabbed him by the arm, but the butcher pulled away.

"Save it," he advised. "I'm not your adversary, Think over what I've said and do whatever you're supposed to do with that chunk of boot-filler. And I'll advise you to do it quick, before Chavorlem catches up with you. Now I'm off."

Alone again, almost against his will, Towler did think. Reluctantly, he had to admit to himself that he had behaved badly and even irrationally. And what if he had? He was under strain enough.

Wearily he got up. Let this thing be finished as soon as possible. Tomorrow he would have no opportunity for speaking to Synvoret all day. A little resolution now might save him much trouble later.

Moving rapidly, Towler wrapped the foot again and stowed it away in the bottom of his deepfreeze. He would approach the Signatory this evening; it was still not late. If he stressed the importance of the matter, no reason existed why Synvoret should not come with his escort straight away to look at the exhibit. Then he could tackle the problem of finding where Elizabeth had gone.

Clamping his faceplate shut, Towler hurried back through the streets, showed his pass at the palace gate, and entered. Shooting up through the building by express lift, he emerged close by the signatorial suite.

As he approached it, the main door opened. Commissioner Par-Chavorlem emerged, his comb erect.

"If you're looking for the Signatory," he said, "I must tell you he is no longer here. I think you had better come with me, Towler. Something has just occurred about which I must speak to you."

XII

Signatory Synvoret rang for Gazer Roifullery and his secretary. They appeared, flattening their combs respectfully.

"It looks as if we shall be allowed little chance of private discussion tomorrow," he said. "So this seems the best opportunity for us to pool our impressions of what we have seen. Half of our time on Earth is up. Let us weigh what evidence we have. Secretary, record the discussion, please."

Roifullery and the secretary lowered their bulks into chairs, the former asking as he did so, "What point would you like to discuss first?"

"Let us begin with this business of our interpreter. Something fishy there, I think you'll agree."

"I would like to, sir, but I confess I don't. That the creature has nothing to say means little or nothing."

"Indeed? My feeling is it means the biped has been bought. Or threatened."

"My feeling is frankly that this interpreter is a fool," Roifullery said. "He cannot even answer questions. Even the amazingly generous offer of your Starjjan land seemed not to move him."

"That might be the response of someone already loaded with care. You don't know these bipeds as I do, Roifullery. My estimation is that he is heavily bribed by Chaverlem Par-Chavorlem."

"Two objections to that, sir," the P-WB man said briskly. "First, if this Towler were really a pawn of the Commissioner's, the Commissioner is clever enough to pick a more polished actor. Secondly, and it's not quite the *ad hominem* argument it sounds, you have come here eager to find something amiss, consequently you find evidence where none exists."

"I am anxious only to find the truth...No, you may be right, Roifullery. When a nul says he wants only the truth, he is generally after a confirmatory truth."

"I am sure I am right, Signatory, with all respects. I am for instance quite prepared to take at its face value Towler's statement that he was not functioning properly at Ashkar because he was scared. I admit I was a little alarmed myself."

Synvoret raised his arm and sighed.

"Now *you* are finding evidence where none exists. You are being oversubtle, Roifullery."

"No sir, *you* are being oversubtle. I have discovered nothing on Earth yet but the need to deal firmly with the local population."

Neither of them were displeased with this exchange. The rules of formal dignatorial behaviour, which they never voluntarily transgressed, allowed them to be frank in passing opinions about each other without at the same time giving offence.

Synvoret rose, ignited a tapering sulphette, and strolled around the room, smoking and thinking aloud.

"We are becoming sidetracked. Let's think of this problem in historical terms. Subject races, whether conquered by arms or treaties, are not notoriously fond of alien rulers. The tyranny they would accept by vote from their own kind without noticing seems to drop oppression when imposed by foreigners.

"In theory, this sense of grievance should be aggravated when the foreigners are of different shape, size and constitution. In practice, it is lessened. The philosophers of Partussy say that this is because subconscious sexual jealousy between conquered and conquerers is absent in such circumstances. However this may be, the Empire is established on this interesting fact.

"It enables us to impose peace on the one hand, and to enrich ourselves on the other. Intrinsically peaceful races accept our rule, warlike ones take more time to knuckle under. This means that one way of solving our problem of what is really happening on Earth is to find out how warlike terrestials actually are. We have an equation in which the other unknown, our X quantity, is exploitation. Are terrestials too unruly, or is Par-Chavorlem digging too much out of them on the side?"

"On the surface," Gazer Roifullery said, "they appear warlike. Not only do they attack our bases – Ashkar, for example – but they indulge in civil wars. I should say that in the circumstances this shows a peculiar aptitude for trouble."

Synvoret nodded.

"That's their herd psychology possibly. Yet as individuals they seem peaceable, you must agree. There is no trouble here in the palace, or in the City. Towler, as we know, is all too quiet."

"You are thinking of them as victims, sir. I think of them as potentially vicious. Towler for instance *seems* quiet enough –"

"A pathetic little creature, Roifullery. Victim material."

"Maybe. So is a wasp. The fellow you spoke to on the street when you arrived; he sounded peaceable enough."

"I have thought about that conversation, Roifullery, and played it back several times on the recorder. It does not ring true. Even the way the creature suddenly appeared was odd. If, and I concede it looks like a big if, Par-Chavorlem is running a virtual dictatorship here, then this creature may have been a pawn of the secret police."

"Unlikely, sir. We have no evidence whatsoever of secret police activity here. As you know, your secretary has checked carefully for the usual evidences of such activity and found none."

"Maybe. Nevertheless, the possibility exists. We need more data, Roifullery. I want you to come out with me and be present when I speak to another biped. I wish you to observe for yourself, and see if your belief in the Commissioner's genial goodness is not shaken."

"Now, sir? It's getting late."

"I trust you are not feeling tired, Gazer?"

The Psycho-Watch nul rose. At Synvoret's suggestion, they both put on air suits. Collecting Raggball, the bodyguard, they went together unobserved, leaving the palace by a side gate as the Signatory had done before.

At this time of day, the streets of the Commission were comparatively crowded. Partussians were returning to their quarters from work or shopping, or else visiting cafés for refreshment. Terrestials were similarly dispersing, or else returning in temporary work details to the outside world. Gaiety was noticeably absent from the atmosphere. But gaiety was not a quality the nuls recognized.

By following some of the terrestials who lived inside the city, the three Partussians arrived at the native quarter. No other of their species were in sight here. Confronted by these narrow streets, tiny shops and shrunken blocks of apartments, all fitted with their half-blisters of airlocks, all three felt something of the excitement of tourists. Here was local colour, here was quaintness! Here lived creatures who breathed diluted oxygen, that curious gas with too many chemical affinities, as if it were as emotional as the creatures dependent on it. For a moment it was impossible to regard the bipeds as other than a peepshow, put on for the convenience and possible edification of Partussy's sons! Indeed, what else could be the purpose behind the whole universe? Did not the Trinity create nul in his-her-its own image?

The Signatory sighed nostalgically, recalling his youth on Starjj.

Most of the terrestials hustled inconspicuously away at the sight of the aliens. One, however, walked towards them, nodding as he passed close by.

"Forgive me, do you speak Partussian?" Synvoret asked.

"Naturally," the man replied. "I am an Under-Oiler at the Mercantile Export Stores. Such a position requires a Proficiency Standard in your language."

"Then perhaps we may speak with you?"

"I am at your service, and pleased to be."

The Signatory and the P-WB nul exchanged glances. Here was another peace-loving terrestial.

"We are travellers from Partussy with only a few days to pass on your world," Synvoret explained. "Naturally we would like a first-hand account of life here. Is there somewhere we can talk together comfortably?"

The terrestial hesitated.

"My room is near," he said. "It is only poor and small, but it could accommodate two of the three of you. Can we go there, since you have air suits on?"

Agreeing, they followed him, snapping tight the domes of their suits as the airlock of the block was reached. Raggball was left outside when his superiors entered.

The scale of the terrestial building was so small for the Partussians that they squeezed in only with difficulty. Inside, the flats were flimsy and depressing. The whole place was without decoration, while the need to conserve air had kept window space down to an absolute minimum. A barracklike hall downstairs provided a sort of recreation room. The rest of the building was given over to corridors, stairs and rooms. Negotiating the stairs with difficulty, while all bipeds fled at their approach, the ill-assorted party arrived at Room 388. The terrestial produced a key and opened up.

Inside, the two Partussians had to sit on the floor, their combs almost touching the ceiling, while the Under-Oiler perched between them. His face had grown very pale. Sweat gathered on his forehead and ran down his cheeks.

"This is hospitable of you," Roifullery said, irritated by this manifestation of emotion. "I take it you feel some friendship for our race?"

"Yes, indeed, nothing but respect," the man said, mopping his face. "When I was taken ill with a throat cancer a little while ago your doctors saved my life. Yes, yes, nothing but respect – and affection."

"Yet you appear," Synvoret observed, "to be terrified of us. Or is it your recent illness which makes you perspire so freely?"

The Under-Oiler gulped. He fished an aphrohale from his pocket, tweaking its end alight with nervous fingers to gain a moment's respite.

"You are very big," he said.

"Do you fancy we may harm you?"

"I – I – I have not yet fully recovered from my illness."

"Should you then be smoking that thing?" asked Synvoret, indicating the aphrohale.

The Under-Oiler looked about him almost desperately.

"Habit," he said. "A bad habit. I'm only a Third Grade worker. . . ."

Roifullery took up the conversation.

"We all have our bad habits. Partussians, you know, inhale things called sulphettes. All intelligent life forms are much alike under their different shapes and skins. Yet you must be tired of our rule on Earth."

"No, sir. Oh no, not at all. We bipeds appreciate the way your species has brought peace all over the galaxy."

"Ha!" Synvoret exclaimed. This fellow spoke as did the

94

native he had first interrogated in the street. Again he asked himself, how could a humble member of an isolated 5c culture, a Third Grade worker at that, think of itself in such terms? What should it know or care of peace in the galaxy? The very phrase "we bipeds" violated the inborn egocentricity of such a culture. Again he felt a suspicion that this fellow had been planted on him. Only for a second did the Signatory hesitate.

"Strip off your clothes!" he said.

The terrestial jumped up, backing to the door, almost the whole of which Synvoret immediately covered with one leg.

"Take off your clothes!" he commanded, sudden excitement taking hold of him.

"This we never do, sir," the wretched terrestial stuttered. "Only for going to bed. Please, sir. . . ."

Synvoret reached out a broad, flapperlike arm. Inserting the tip of one digit inside the neck of the terrestial's shirt, he tugged. The terrestial was jerked forward. With a ripping sound his jerkin, shirt and vest were torn. He staggered away, and then Roifullery grabbed him from behind.

As he began to shout for mercy, Roifullery enveloped him in folds of arms, stilling his cries and struggles. The Gazer's comb had sharpened into a down-curling hook.

Synvoret pulled the tattered clothing away from the Under-Oiler's chest, bending an eye-stalk until it functioned as a powerful microscope, he traced from an unobtrusive lump under the biped's left ear a scar that ran to another lump just above his breast bone. From there another scar, invisible to normal eyesight, ran to a third and larger lump above the heart.

As a cat unsheathes its claws, Synvoret unsheathed from his arm a long bladelike claw, remnant of the days, millenia ago, when Partussians were minor predators on an unnamed planet. With this claw, he sliced under the flesh of the biped's breast.

A delicate double thread of wire was revealed, running from heart to throat.

"Let him go," Synvoret said. "That's all we wish to know. My case is proved, Roifullery. This is a typical spy device."

Bleeding and gasping, the biped staggered back as Roifullery released him. It seemed dazed. With ineffectual movements, it sought to pull its tattered clothing around its chest. Tears ran down its face. They glanced at it half fascinated by its display.

"I don't understand. What is this apparatus under its skin?" Roifullery asked.

"Have you Psycho-Watch people no acquaintance with auricle-pumps? This creature has a little transmitter grafted in, which is actually worked by the action of the heart. With leads to his throat and ear, he can communicate with a distant point without anyone else being aware of the fact."

"I've heard of them, but never seen one before," Roifullery admitted, adding with some reluctance, "I believe they are typical secret police tools, aren't they?"

"Of course they are. Let's get back to the palace."

Ignoring the biped, who still whimpered from fright and pain, they pushed out of the room. Synvoret felt a certain shame – an unusual experience for a nul, whose behaviour was closely governed by the frigid situation-response selector it called conscience. He was aware how much he and the Gazer had relished their power over the little biped. Thrusting the sensation behind him, clamping down his airdome, he led the way from the block of apartments.

As he did so, Arm Marshall Terekomy, in a hidden room in Police HQ, snapped off a receiver.

Crossing at a run to a soundproof booth, he was speaking to Par-Chavorlem within thirty seconds.

"Synvoret's out on another native hunt," he said. "He's just returning."

"I know. I've been to his suite and found him out. We agreed he should be free to do this."

"Of course we did. But listen, he's a crafty devil! I put a C 309 on to him. He took Synvoret and the P-WB nul up to his room and started to propagandize as instructed. Then Synvoret cut him up and found the auricle-pump! I heard every word over C 309's transmitter. How he guessed the biped was wired is beyond me – it repeated very carefully everything we told it to say."

"What's happening now?" Par-Chavorlem's voice asked. As ever, it was gentle and unhurried.

"They're both coming back to the palace, convinced they have all tabs on us. Huh! So they have! Now they've definite grounds for suspicion, we'll never keep control –"

"Don't lose your comb, Terekomy. Here's what you must do immediately."

Less than two minutes later, the first of a stream of ambulances began to roar in the streets of the City, its alarm note sounding.

XIII

Before Terekomy's urgent interruption came, the Commissioner was speaking to Towler

"I brought you here to ask you some questions. See you answer them straightforwardly."

"I shall do my best," Towler said. All his nerves were tense. The friendly façade that Par-Chavorlem had tried to preserve for the last few days had vanished. In its place was a formidable animal in a uniform, ten feet high, and of considerable strength and cunning. Not only that. This particular animal had almost unlimited power over all the other creatures on this planet, except for one. And that one was Synvoret, not Towler.

"Stand on that chair so I can see your face levelly when you answer me," Par-Chavorlem ordered.

There was nothing for it but to obey. Towler climbed on to the big nul chair and faced his adversary.

"Better. Now, Interpreter, I'm getting a lot of trouble from your branch. It was Chettle and Wedman the other day. Now the woman interpreter, Fallodon, has disappeared. You know of this, of course?"

"Of course."

"We can find no trace of her as yet."

One of the Commissioner's eye-stalks extended telescopically, examining Towler from close range. Its end came to within a foot of Towler's air helmet, and a cold grey orb surveyed him.

"Unfortunately in this temporary City I am less in touch with what goes on than I should be," Par-Chavorlem continued. "But from visi-records from the old City I know that you have been increasingly intimate with Fallodon over the last two years. Is that correct?"

"Yes."

"Then you know her well. Where has she gone?"

Towler moistened his lips. He knew trouble was coming.

"I don't know, sir. I wish I did know."

"You should know. I made you Chief Interpreter, you are in charge of her."

"I was with the Signatory when she disappeared."

"So? Then where has she gone? Is she dead?"

"I hope not."

"You hope not! Why do you hope not?"

". . . I love her, sir."

At this the Commissioner let out a bellow of fury. One of his broad arms caught Towler and forced him back over the arm of the chair, pressing against his chest. Towler's helmet plate fogged over, and he was in a misty world of his own, although that angry unmetaphorical language still roared outside it.

"You speak to me of love, that whimsy madness no triped tolerates in his system! This filthy planet! How can it ever run or be run efficiently with imponderables like love in it? I'll show you what Partussy thinks of such weakness. Get up. Hurry up, get up."

Towler had the knife under his tunic. He could not kill this great cylinder of hateful blubber, yet he might be able to slash off one of its eye-stalks before he was dashed to the ground. Then he realized he could not draw the knife without letting into his suit the stinking poison of Partussian air. Gasping heavily, he rose and again faced his enemy who was now just visible through his clearing face plate. Par-Chavorlem's comb was compressed with rage.

"Find out about Fallodon. I give you till tomorrow night to discover details of what has happened to her."

"Your spies can do better than I can."

"You think so? Perhaps they don't have the personal interest you have. You find out what's happened to her. Now get out."

Choking with baffled anger, Towler made towards the door. When he had his hand on its latch, Par-Chavorlem called him back.

"You know why I'm interested in Fallodon, don't you, Towler? Because I suspect that puny fool Rivars has an agent in the palace. She may be the agent. Fallodon would be amenable to my sort of questioning on the subject, I think."

"Miss Fallodon has not been out of the City since she was brought to it by force two years ago. It's nonsense to suppose she knows anything about Rivars."

"We'll see. I tell you this, Towler: nothing shall go wrong while Synvoret is here. If it does, you will die for one, and I swear I'll burn out or bring into captivity every single biped on the planet. Before I made you fair promises. Now I make you only threats. Get out, and come back here tomorrow with useful information."

As Towler left the study, Par-Chavorlem's emergency bell rang. It was his call from Terekomy. Blind to everything, even the sympathetic glances of other interpreters, Towler went home to sleep. All night long, dreams blew through his skull like newspaper down an empty street, waking him at last to a new day and a sharpened sense of doom.

Synvoret, on the other hand, woke from a *jarm*-induced slumber to a new sense of contentedness. He believed he had at last gained an insight into the question of Earth. His work here, he felt, was almost done, and it was with an easy mind he entered into his host's arrangements for a day's hunting.

As they sped out from the City, along one of the great roads through a world still in darkness, owing to the different lengths of City and planetary day, Synvoret reflected on the events of the night before, after he and Roifullery had uncovered the Third Grade worker's auricle-pump.

They had returned to the palace to find a certain amount of controlled excitement everywhere. Ignoring this at first, Synvoret had gone straight to Par-Chavorlem and spoken gravely.

"Commissioner, I must ask to see you alone."

"Certainly, Signatory, but first please allow me to settle some urgent business," the Commissioner said, flattening his comb. "I very much regret that a dangerous madman is loose in the native quarter. Our men are making every effort to track him down, and I must go over to the hospital and be of what assistance I can. Perhaps you would care to come? No doubt you heard the ambulances in the street."

"I certainly heard ambulances," Synvoret said with reserve. He and Roifullery exchanged glances.

"They were collecting a poor Earthian, a harmless Third Grade Under-Oiler, who has been brutally attacked by an assailant or assailants unknown. He is in hospital now. I hold it my duty to go and see him. It is terrible this sort of thing should happen. It merely shows how unstable these bipeds are."

And Synvoret, with growing curiosity and uncertainty, had accompanied the Commissioner to the hospital. There he found the man whose auricle-pump he had exposed only a short while before, lying in a bed unconscious. Again he felt a rush of

99

shame. A part of him whispered that it had been a pleasure to rip up this helpless creature, that there had been a prurient joy in watching it so openly emote. Then he silenced this voice. After all, whatever he had felt, he had been doing his duty.

But the pause lost Synvoret the initiative. He hesitated, and thereby gave his opponent the chance of winning his bluff. He could not now admit that he was himself responsible for this injury.

"They are poor frail things, bipeds," said Par-Chavorlem heavily.

"What's the matter with him?" asked Synvoret.

Par-Chavorlem explained how this hospital was one of the most advanced in Sector Vermilion and how by adapting an abhorred secret police weapon for humanitarian ends they had produced a means of keeping in constant touch with their ailing patients. Unctiously, he described how this poor wretch had had a throat disease coupled with severe mental disorder, and how he was responding to the new medical treatment, whereby such information as heartbeat rate and nervous activity was automatically registered in, and controlled by, the hospital wherever the sufferer might be.

It was a very convincing tale.

He then took the Signatory to another chamber in the building where medical nuls and men bent over instruments, assimilating data on other out-patients as it came in.

That too was very convincing.

Par-Chavorlem and Terekomy had worked fast and well. Synvoret, if not entirely converted, was suitably deceived, accusing himself of too readily jumping to conclusions.

"What will happen to this biped who was attacked?" he inquired, when the charade was over and they had left the flickering dials and white coats behind.

"We hope he will recover. Unfortunately, his nerves have undergone a grave shock. He was unconscious when discovered and has remained so. Even more unfortunately, our investigators have uncovered some evidence which tends to show he was attacked by a Partussian, or rather two Partussians. My deepest regret is that this should happen while you are visiting us. I would like to assure you that when we catch these two dangerous tripeds they will be dealt with with the full severity of the law. I take a grave view of inter-species violence."

"Hm ... Yes, I see," said Synvoret, feeling extremely uncomfortable. It was already too late and too complicated for him to try and explain.

He was not unsubtle. The thought did occur to him that Par-Chavorlem might be bluffing, although his story and the circumstantial evidence backing it was perfectly convincing. But if it were so, his silent acquiescence, had now placed him in the Commissioner's hands. Should he do other than silently acquiesce, then it was within the Par-Chavorlem's power to see that the biped died and the names of his murderers were announced. From the distance of Partussy, the whole business would look sordid in the extreme, and he would die with his name under a cloud.

This was not a line of thought he pursued for long. The demonstration Par-Chavorlem and Terekomy had rigged for him at the hospital was too thorough.

"I have been unjust to Par-Chavorlem all along. I came here biased with a case to prove against him," the Signatory told himself as he bowled through the Earthly dawn. So ran his conscious reasoning. Below it, reinforcing it and unknown to him, was a growing sense of guilt about his treatment of terrestials, which he could only suppress by regarding them as beyond rational compassion. Thus is the psychology of the oppressor tempered.

From then on his attitude hardened. Increasingly, he was Par-Chavorlem's dupe.

They reached a hunting lodge in the Northern Administrative Division of Cumbland. This lodge was owned by the powerful family of Par-Junt, distant relations of Par-Chavorlem's. Their welcome was courteous and sincere, their attention to the Signatory hospitable and gentle. During the day the party between them shot over three hundred wild *affrizzians*.

When they returned to the City late that evening, Synvoret was full of pleasure. He retired early, forgetting he had wished to see Towler and hear any confidential revelations he might wish to make.

Par-Chavorlem had not forgotten his appointment with Towler.

After he had checked over the events of the day with Terekomy, he rang for the chief interpreter.

Towler was pale but defiant when he arrived.

"I have no news of Miss Fallodon. She has disappeared

completely. You'd better ask your Arm Marshall about her. Perhaps he has her in one of his secret cells."

Terekomy's comb folded sideways.

"Take care of your tongue, biped," he warned.

"So you cannot or will not help us," said Par-Chavorlem. He turned to a nul guard behind him. "Bring in the prisoner."

A rear door was thrown open. A nul bore in a human figure strapped to a pole, setting it upright so that the figure stood willy-nilly. Through the face plate, Towler saw the frightened countenance of his butcher. At once his heart began to hammer with trepidation.

"You know who this is," Terekomy said to Towler. "He was seen with you going to your flat yesterday."

"He is a friend of mine," Towler said.

"A good friend, no doubt. Speak to him in your language, ask him about Fallodon."

Towler turned to the butcher, bitterness filling him. Changing from Partussian to his native tongue he said, "I got you into this trouble by my own foolishness. I must have been mad! What can I say? What can I do? I'd rather I was there than you."

"It's just luck. It's not your fault." He spoke painfully. "These horrors have ruined me, crushed my stomach in, I shouldn't wonder. You know their sort of questioning."

"You've told them everything?"

"Not on your life! You're in the clear...." He paused, sighed, then continued with obvious effort. "All I told 'em was a bit of hearsay, that a driver told me Elizabeth Fallodon had smuggled herself out of the City. Weak fool I was! The driver and four others are dead by now, on account of my babbling tongue."

"Out of the City! You mean she was trying to contact –"

"Yes, you know who. Your pal. So at least if she's safe –"

"All right!" Terekomy interrupted, setting himself between Towler and the butcher. "Don't jabber all day. What did he say about Fallodon, Interpreter?"

Towler hesitated.

"That she's got away from you. She's not dead, she's free, thank God."

Par-Chavorlem slammed an arm on to the desk top.

"And you didn't know that? You still pretend you had nothing to do with it? You –"

"No. No, I swear."

"So much for love –" The Commissioner was suddenly quiet. Then he turned to the uniformed nul who held the butcher upright on his pole.

"Guard, smash that biped's faceplate," he ordered.

"No!" Towler cried. He threw himself forward, but Terekomy seized him.

"Tell the truth," he said, "if you want your friend's life spared. You knew about Fallodon. She's taking a message to Rivars for you, isn't she?"

"No! No!" Towler shouted again, so loudly he never heard the butcher's faceplate cracked. Only the man's coughing silenced him, a broken cough that went on and on, stopping only to start again, until it was finally quieted for ever in the thick Partussian atmosphere.

Par-Chavorlem was the first to speak. He had watched the dying man's gestures with interest.

"Towler, after this I am forced to believe you are not guilty of what we suspected. This pleases me, since very few terrestials have your grasp of our beautiful and intricate language. However, you are to a certain extent implicated with terrestials who are guilty. You are a fool if not a knave. So, you are demoted from the post of Chief Interpreter herewith. From tomorrow you will join the ordinary interpreter's pool. You will not speak to Signatory Synvoret again. Interpreter Peter Lardening will take over your post. Now get out and send Lardening in to me. Move."

Limply, Towler went out. Shock and horror made him quake in every limb; the butcher's groans still echoed in his ears. The only shred of comfort in the whole business was that Elizabeth had obviously escaped. And her going was proof of her love for him rather than the reverse, she had gone before the Starjjan foot arrived, no doubt to fetch the evidence herself from Rivars.

One thing Towler promised himself. As soon as this crisis was over, and before Chav had them all back among the unfightable restrictions of the other City, he would break out and find Elizabeth. He needed her more than anything.

Meanwhile, Towler still had the Starjjan foot. But it would be harder now than ever to find an opportunity for presenting it to the visiting Signatory Synvoret.

XIV

The next day was the fifth day of Synvoret's visit.

For Towler it passed fruitlessly. Confined to the interpreter's pool, translating numerous and irrelevant Vermilion bulletins into English, he hardly saw a nul all day.

At least it was a minor relief from tension to be accepted back by his old friends. Wearily, he briefed Peter Lardening for his new role as well as he could. That young man was also showing signs of strain, but Towler recalled his fondness for Elizabeth, and could only sympathize.

Synvoret, today with only Terekomy in attendance to show him the things he ought to see, investigated several sub-commissions and visited, with a heavy guard, the curious old terrestial city of London, where several thousands of bipeds and not a few nul archaeologists still lived.

Lardening reported on the trip in the off-duty room that evening.

"The old fool's sold on the Empire way of life," he said. "There's not a chance of his seeing through Chav's bluff now. We were mad to expect he'd ever be any help to us."

"How was my dismissal explained to him?" Towler asked. "Didn't he think that was curious?"

"Not a bit of it. Chav had a tale, of course. He told Synvoret he had discovered you had not interpreted truthfully what the refugees said at Ashkar. According to him they were really saying how much they hated Rivars and his terrorists. And Synvoret believed it!"

"We have two and a half days left!" Towler cried in agony.

"What can you do? Synvoret would no longer know the truth if he heard it."

"Something must be done. You're the one in contact with him now, Lardening. You'd better think of something."

As he spoke, Towler looked around at the other interpreters. There were half a dozen of them, Reonachi, Spadder, Johns, Eugene, Klee and Meller, anxiously gathered to see what was going on at a time of crisis. These were the men who had condemned his behaviour. Now their faces saddened Towler. They were helpless. If they had hope, it was the spineless hope that someone else would do something. They were the end products of a thousand years of Partussian rule; a subject race.

It forced Towler to see himself in a new light. He had endured much, and that in constant apprehension. But at least he could and would endure. He had the one thing these men lacked; resolution.

Slapping Lardening reassuringly on the back, he left. The joy of accepting a challenge was in him.

Towler woke to the sixth day of Synvoret's visit with his new determination still in command.

He thought first of all of Rivars. According to latest reports, the leader was now engaged in a fierce battle with the Starjjan force among the desolate slopes of the Varne Heights. Nevertheless, Rivars would have time to worry about the delivery of his evidence to Synvoret, which had now been in Towler's deepfreeze for almost three days.

By nightfall it must be in the Signatory's hands.... But how?

Luck seemed to be with Towler. As he finished breakfast an urgent call came through for him. He lifted the receiver and replied.

"Palace here, Gary. Come over fast, will you? Peter Lardening's been taken ill. Synvoret has asked for you back today, and he's due to leave for a sight of the battle line in twenty minutes."

"I'll be there."

He put the instrument down slowly. Curious! Lardening had looked fit enough last evening. Well, it looked as if a chance to speak to Synvoret alone would be more easily come by than he had dared hope for. Squaring his shoulders, he started out for the palace – not without wishing that his dear Elizabeth could see him in his new role of hero!

Both Synvoret and Roifullery were amiable but silent, not relishing the prospect of a brief air journey. Stoically, like good nuls, they climbed into a survey ship with Terekomy and Par-Chavorlem. The latter merely gave Towler an admonitory nod of his comb, as if to say, "Just dare try anything while I'm about...."

The ship took off, rose through the overhead lock and into the Earth's atmosphere. Wheeling it turned south-east towards the contested Varne Heights.

Once at its objective, it hovered inside cumulus cloud, five thousand feet above the ground. Through infra-vision, the Partussians in the ship could watch the activity on the land below, where a large party of Starjjans were attempting to reach a smaller group of their kind who had been cut off along a hill ridge by patriot forces. Picked out by telescopes, the tiny figures crawled like lice over a rumpled counterpane, their actions interesting for a while but without significance.

To Synvoret, of course, they were merely terrestials squabbling with terrestials. He was taking the godlike view.

"Seeing this sort of barbarism makes me more than ever aware that we Partussians have a mission in the galaxy," he said.

"I wonder, Signatory, if you do not think me too lenient with the bipeds," Par-Chavorlem said smoothly. "I know my responsibility is to keep peace, yet it seems the greater wisdom to leave these creatures to sort out their own indistinguishable differences. It is the wisest way to avoid any possible animosity against ourselves."

Synvoret meditated only for a second.

"I think you maintain a fair rule," he said. "The more I see, the more I'm convinced of it."

Towler, the only terrestial sitting with these huge beings, sighed wretchedly. Hour by hour, Synvoret was becoming more confirmed in Par-Chavorlem's point of view. Already he believed the Commissioner's rule was just. Soon he would be capable of applauding injustice to the wretched bipeds.

Again Towler thought, *I'm the one human who sees how things are shaping. I must keep, if possible, to Rivars' plan, but is it any longer the best one?* And once more he reviewed his doubts of Rivars' abilities. The whole business was becoming less manageable as time went on.

Looking at the featureless turret of the Partussian Signatory's head, Towler could not help wishing that the survey ship would suddenly fall from the cloud and crash, killing everyone it contained – including himself. It would solve his problems at least.

Synvoret soon grew tired of peering down at the storming of an insignificant hillside.

"Have we not seen enough of these squabbling bipeds?" he asked. "Can we not turn for home?"

"The men down there are fighting for their lives and their

ideals!" Towler almost blurted out suddenly, moved to anger by the contempt implicit in the other's words.

But he was quiet. He realized now that in spite of the investigation, in spite of the search for justice, these visitors were nuls. And nuls found it difficult to understand bipeds. Add to that the cleverness and thoroughness of Par-Chavorlem. . . .

Towler did not look at them. He had decided already that he must kill Synvoret. No other action would release the burning hatred in his breast.

XV

They were back in the City in time for lunch. Towler, eating in the Terrestial Staff Mess, had little appetite. Lardening did not appear, although Meller reported that he was better. The interpreters frequently went down with a twelve hour fever they called "nul sickness," brought on mainly by the restricted conditions under which they had to work.

The rest of the day passed in dull routine, as Towler followed the party of nuls around City House.

Synvoret and Gazer Roifullery, with various Commission officials in attendance, spent much time investigating the governmental machinery, which consisted chiefly of an actual machine, the Recorder, in which all details of expenditure and income from the City, the sub-commissions, and other sources were stored. Since, as Towler suspected, the figures were rigged in the first place, the investigators learnt nothing untoward from them. Only Par-Chavorlem knew Earth's true profit and loss account. The inspection, indeed, grew more and more cursory. When one of the officials suggested drinks and sulphettes, Synvoret was happy to agree.

The party moved into a private room, leaving Towler to wait outside.

Waiting, he thought over his next move.

His new courage had something of desperation in it. Whatever he was going to do must be done very soon.

Rivars had indicated he had other terrestials working for him secretly in the palace. By now Rivars would know he had not acted as instructed, and would be growing impatient. He would probably presume that Towler had sold out to the highest bidder – Synvoret or Par-Chavorlem. If he presumed that, his next move was predictable. He would instruct his other palace agents to exterminate Towler.

The idea made Towler's flesh crawl. Again he had the strange feeling that Rivars was enemy rather than ally. Well, he must act. At the same time, he must act for reasons other than self-preservation.

The main reason was simple. Ever since his meeting with Rivars, Towler had doubted the patriot leader's judgement. Now that doubt flared into active mistrust. Rivars was a soldier, one having no knowledge of the finesse of diplomacy, particularly such diplomacy as Partussy fostered. Rivars thought of the Signatory as a sort of Saviour figure; a man of knowledge and integrity who would find the truth and proclaim it. Synvoret fell ludicrously short of that estimate.

Supposing I produced the webbed Starjjan foot for Synvoret. Will that worthy be able, from the depths of his sophistry, to discount it? Will he not dismiss it perhaps as the foot of a terrestial freak, or believe that it has somehow been smuggled illegally into the planet to prove a case?

No, Rivars' ingenious piece of evidence seems no longer effective as once it did, now that Synvoret is virtually in Par-Chavorlem's pocket.

It followed that anything offered to Synvoret might be rejected. How then to get the truth about Earth back to the Colony Worlds Council in the Queen World?

One way only presented itself: by killing Synvoret.

Synvoret was an important member of the Council. His death on an almost unknown planet would create an uproar. As soon as possible, another team of investigators – and this time probably military men – would arrive to investigate affairs both on Earth and its supervisory planet, Castacorze, Vermilion HQ. They would be definitely looking for trouble, and they would find it. Indeed, they would probably want Par-Chavorlem for a scapegoat whether he was guilty or not.

It was clear that Synvoret could be of no help to Earth now unless he was dead. And Towler must kill him.

Two days ago this might have been unthinkable. Now it was even pleasurable. All the same, killing one of these giant tripeds, who had so few vulnerable areas, was a considerable task. Towler had only a knife and determination. He needed also a very favourable opportunity.

108

By the time the Partussian delegation emerged from their drinking party, Towler had a plan improvised.

Approaching the Signatory, he said, "In a room in the vaults of the palace are preserved some of the art treasures created by terrestials before they became a subject race. May I show them to you if you have finished here?"

Synvoret swivelled an eye-stalk at him.

"Do you think your form of art is likely to appeal to me, Interpreter?" he asked.

"Our art took many forms. You have seen that we can be warlike. You ought also to see the fruits of peace."

"Possibly so," the Signatory agreed indifferently. "While I am here I am willing to see anything."

They descended to the art room, only the silent Raggball accompanying them. This, however, was one too many for Towler. If he was to have any chance of success, he must get Synvoret alone.

The store contained treasures from many ages and lands. Most of it was illegally acquired and would be illegally disposed of. As long as the plundered and broken towns of Earth continued to yield up treasure, this room would not be empty. The whole heritage of Earth was gradually being dispersed to nearby worlds, the proceeds going to fill Par-Chavorlem's personal coffers.

Synvoret walked among all this tragic pomp without a word, pausing nowhere, hurrying nowhere, his eye-stalks sweeping continuously from side to side. At last he came back to Towler.

"How can biped art mean anything to other beings?" he asked gently. "It is all superficial, mere outward display, rationalized emotion. I can see nothing here to detain me, though this is not to denigrate its value to you."

"Nothing at all that interests you?"

The Partussian hesitated, towering above the interpreter.

"One thing is interesting and curious," he said, and he led the way stolidly down among the cases and exhibits. He indicated a stiff and shining square of thick material, covered with a simple repeated motif, consisting of a three-armed whirl. The label on its exhibition case said: LINOLEUM. XX CENT. FRENCH. (PARIS?)

"You like this?" Towler asked.

"It is likeable. It seems to me to bear a more exact relationship to the universe than the rest of the work I have examined here."

Towler licked his lips.

"It so happens I have a precisely similar pattern in my private room. The collection of such old treasures is my hobby. Would you come with me to collect it? I feel I would like to present you with it as a gift, to show how much I have enjoyed my brief contact with you as your interpreter. It would be particularly pleasurable to me if this humble ceremony could take place in my room. I have never had a Partussian guest before."

Synvoret appeared to meditate.

"Yes, it might be pleasant." Momentarily he was seeing himself back on Partussy, saying to his friends, *The natives were hospitable in their feeble way. They invited me to their wretched homes, loaded me with gifts....* "Yes, let us go," he said aloud. "It will be convenient for me now."

"My little home is so small that I fear there will be no room in it for Raggball."

Stopping only to collect Partussian air suits, they started for the native quarter and an appointment with death. The stroll held for Towler an air of unreality. He knew that, like an actor in a play, he walked upon a temporary set. This whole Commission had been hastily erected purely for Synvoret's benefit. When – if – he left, it would be abandoned, as Par-Chavorlem ordered everyone back to their old, more capacious city. The gaunt, unpainted buildings were here only for a moment, the backdrop to a drama of deceit upon the success of which depended the future of Earth.

At this time, it was no more than a backdrop. They walked close by the fair, where a few cafés were beginning to open. Towler's perceptions were almost entirely wrapped about himself. He noticed nothing. He had invited Synvoret to his flat only because there his chances of making a kill were increased. There, a rip in the other's air suit could be lethal. Once Synvoret's suit was punctured, he would have to concentrate not upon defence or attack but on survival. And then a well-aimed blow under the arms might kill him.

Leaving Raggball on guard in the street, they entered the airlock, the big Partussian having to squeeze in.

"I must make you feel like a pygmy," he grunted. Towler was too overwrought to manage a reply.

110

In the living room, Synvoret swivelled his eye-stalks expectantly. At these close quarters, in his small room, he looked overwhelming.

Unlatching the front of his helmet, licking his lips, Towler said, "Stay here. The thing's in the kitchen."

Almost blindly, he hurried from the room. Panting, he pulled open a provision cupboard and pulled his antique knife from the back of it, where it had been hidden these last two days. Its handle was of solid wood. The blade, eight inches long, was single-edged, curving to a point. It had been Wedman's knife, and a serviceabe weapon it was. It would do the job.

Thrusting it into his pocket, Towler vacillated again. When he returned to the other room, it was with the Starjjan foot. Though he had little faith in Rivars' orders, he would obey them. He would give the Signatory one last chance, judge his reactions. He set the foot on the table in its frosty wrappings.

"What is this?" Synvoret asked sternly.

"Examine it, sir! You told me once you were after the truth of the situation on Earth. Here's the truth. I brought you here to show it to you. Examine it! Unwrap it!"

He held the knife ready in his pocket as Synvoret peeled back paper and canvas and pulled out the frozen foot.

"Remove this disgusting object at once, Interpreter."

"You can see it's not a human foot, can't you?"

"I have no idea what a human foot looks like, you fool. What are you playing at? Raggball! Raggball!"

As the Signatory shouted for his bodyguard, he swept the foot off the table with a broad arm.

Never for a moment had it occurred to Towler that the Signatory, despite all his years on Starjj, might have no knowledge of the structure of a Starjjan foot. But whether he knew or not, he was unaware of the structure of a terrestial's foot. It was a stupid and unforeseen slice of miscalculation. The unexpectedness of it woke Towler to action.

Bending as if to retrieve the severed foot, he drew his knife. The Partussian had taken fright, was bellowing still for Raggball. Towler had only a moment in which to act.

He stabbed from behind with all his might, dragging the sharp blade down the expanse of suit, seeing it wrinkle and part, smelling the reek of sulphur-hydrogen as it escaped. Then a blow from Synvoret sent him flying. Stumbling head over heels, he dropped the knife and crashed into his bed, half-stunned.

He lay limply against the bed, staring helplessly across the room. Synvoret had moved to the wall, pressing himself against it so that the rip in his suit was at least partially sealed. The knife lay at his great feet. Towler began to crawl towards it, but Synvoret stood ready to lash out again. They glared at each other. It was deadlock until Raggball arrived; neither could harm the other.

They hated in silence, and then the door broke open and the bodyguard burst in.

"Stay here and guard him," Synvoret said. A tremor was apparent in his voice. "Stay here and guard him. I will send reinforcements."

He left hastily as Raggball lumbered over to Towler.

XVI

From Synvoret's point of view, by subjective time, it was eight weeks and two days later when the freighter *Geboraa* landed him and his party back on Partussy in the Queen City. Borne halfway across the galaxy at a speed and in a para-universe where light was a sluggish solid, he had bypassed the two years and several weeks which had lapsed in the ordinary universe. Time contracted to carry him back to Partussy with his memories of Earth intact.

The Colony Worlds Council Hall was packed with signatories and semi-signatories. After the Trinity had been praised, and Synvoret and two other travellers from distant parts of Empire had been welcomed back with a formal speech from the Tripos the general business of the day began. This was an informal general session. The matters dealt with changed little from year to year: infringements of elemental monopolies, trans-sector disputations, ministerial peccadillos, the carthanaxian question, high-level transgressions of galactic rights.

Synvoret was infinitely soothed to hear these familiar problems come up, one by one, only to be resolved in ethico-legal fashion by the signatories best equipped to deal with them. This, he reflected, was the place for him, a soft seat on his home planet. He was too old to go adventuring again. Relaxed, he heard the Master Tripos calling the next item.

"Know this, Assembly, that just returned to Partussy is one Wattol Forlie, dismissed from the post of a Commission Third Secretary on a Class 5c world in GAS Vermilion. This world, namely Earth in System 5417, is under the Commissionership of the High Hiscount Chaverlem Par-Chavorlem, against whom Wattol Forlie does bring the following grave charges. First, highest treason, in that the accused does set the fair name of Partussy into foul repute. Second, ordinary treason, in that the accused does bring his own office into disrepute. . . ."

Now Synvoret was no longer relaxed. He sat tensely listening as his personal secretary took notes beside him. He had not yet made his official report on Earth to the Supreme Councillor, whose private hearings were held only once a month. It was a coincidence merely that this issue should occur in ordinary council session. Wattol Forlie must have reached home at almost the same time as the Signatory.

". . . Third, corruption, in that the accused does deploy his forces for his own personal gain. Fourth, exploitation, in that the accused manoeuvres the subject race under him for his own personal gain. . . ."

The list of charges increased. There were nine in all. At length the Master Tripos looked up and said, in the traditional parlance of the council, "Let he who brings these charges show himself to the assembly and vouch that the intention is of his own, and Trinity and Empire not abused thereby."

A figure rose some distance from Synvoret and announced cockily, "Here I am, gentlemen, ladies, neuters. The intention is mine and I am pursuivant of it. And I'll tell you I'd never have got here for years yet, if some good traveller on a filthy dump called Appelobetnees III hadn't given me nine tens for a prize-winning lottery ticket. That bit of luck paid my way home."

"That is sufficient," cried the Tripos. "The charges can speak for themselves. So you are present, so you hold silence."

A ripple of amusement ran around the chamber, quickly hushed as the speaker continued. "Who shall sift these matters in preliminary or in toto? Stand up and speak all signatories with special and relevant knowledge of the matters contained in these charges."

Only Synvoret rose.

"The staggering total of nine charges. This dismissed Third Secretary must have hired an able lawyer!"

113

These, his first words, brought a mutter of amusement from his fellows, in which a note of welcome revealed their pleasure in seeing a cherished face back among them. Though at present he was intellectually unprepared to make a statement, suddenly he was emotionally ready. He had done his state some service; there remained one duty to perform. Unexpectedly, he found himself full of words.

"Signatories all," he began. "This matter touches very closely on the Investigation from which I have just returned. A full and proper report of it will go to the Supremo at the month's end. Meanwhile, I will briefly give you the gist of my judgements as they affect the charge. Most of you will not have heard of Earth. I have visited it. I have just come back from there. Grave allegations from this same source against one of our Commissioners, Par-Chavorlem, have already come to my attention. I went to Earth with the express purpose of investigating them."

He was a noble figure standing there. He was well-known and well-liked. Nobody listening doubted his integrity. Synvoret was one of the old guard, beyond self-interest and corruption. One glance at the ancient splendour of his coat told you that.

"Let me deal with the indictment charge by charge," he continued. "The first charge of highest treason. This charge, I suggest, cannot operate until the dismissed Third Secretary Forlie has produced corroborative charges from a higher source. Highest treason can only be committed against higher sources. Castacorze, Sector Vermilion HQ would be, for instance, a higher source in Par-Chavorlem's case, but they have brought no such charge against him.

"The second charge of ordinary treason. To my personal knowledge, Par-Chavorlem does not bring his office into disrepute. I spoke during my stay to Partussian landowners of the highest repute – the name of the Par-Junt family will be familiar to you – and these good people hold the Commissioner in the greatest esteem and affection. Even the bipeds regard him with affection. I was *there*, gentlemen, meeting these creatures face to face. The bipeds of Earth wage civil wars with brother killing brother. I went out on to their battlefields and spoke with them personally, uncensoredly. I well remember on one occasion going right into a forward area, a town called Ashkar where fighting had been going on for weeks, where we were constantly under nuclear bombardment. A stream of biped refugees –"

He was interrupted by a question from the Middle Phalanx.

"Do we understand the Signatory to say that Commissioner Par-Chavorlem allowed him to enter a position of physical danger? Surely that was very lax of him?"

"He was helping me in my investigation. He quite understood that it was my duty to go everywhere and see everything. May I continue? Refugees were streaming past us at this terrible place. I remember speaking to one poor old lady who had lost everything she had. Her relations had been killed, her home destroyed. She was turning naturally to the Commission as a place of friendliness and shelter in which she might live out the rest of her days. I remember her very words, 'The Commission's the only safe place for me, sir.' "

There was an interruption from a Dlotpodite, a triped species which had gradually climbed from the status of satellites to near-equals of Partussians.

"Do you personally speak the terrestial language, Signatory?"

"Naturally not, but –"

"Do you recall if Commissioner Par-Chavorlem does?"

"Er, no, naturally he does not either; you see, there is no terrestial language, only a series of dialects with which no serious nul could trouble himself. These bipeds are very primitive, you understand; they have had the benefit of only a thousand years of our supervision. May I please continue? On the third charge of corruption. Of this, I and the officer from Psycho-Watch who accompanied me, Gazer Roifullery, found absolutely no evidence. The records were all faultlessly in order. Needless to say, we investigated them ourselves. And as a minor example of the Commissioner's punctiliousness, I can say that I examined a large chamber full of art treasures of Earth which Par-Chavorlem keeps under his care, no doubt against the day when the terrestials develop enough responsibility to look after them themselves. If he was as corrupt as this foolish charge claims, why did he not sell the treasures?"

"The fourth charge of exploitation. . . ."

Synvoret paused. This council, who would later investigate his investigatory team's findings when the Supremo had passed them, must be given the general picture as vividly as possible.

How could he tell them most clearly about a world none of them would ever see or wish to *see*?

He thought back to his crowded days on Earth, recalling various incidents. One above all stayed in his mind.

"I went to Earth," he said, "with my usual sympathy for a subject race, determined that it should have fair treatment. I found an emotionally unstable species for whom violence is irresistible. Chavorlem is more lenient with it than it deserves. He does not exploit it enough. Driven harder it would fight less. Why, these bipeds are beyond reason!" Synvoret was gripping his desk now, his comb erect, speaking so compulsively from memory that the whole assembly hung on his words. They were carried along by the fervour with which he spoke. "There was one biped with whom I had actually been, as I imagined, fairly intimate. He was my interpreter. I even condescended to visit his room in Commission City. He promised to give me a farewell present, but when we were alone, with absolutely no provocation, he tried to murder me, to stab me! It was a savage, cowardly attack. Only by using my wits did I escape death."

All around the vast council chamber sounded murmurs of horror and sympathy. The insistent voice of the Dlotpodite came again, "Why was Par-Chavorlem lax enough to allow a killer in the City?" but momentarily it was drowned in an uproar of admiration as the massed signatories expressed their warmth for a nul who had ventured his life in the cause of justice.

This grand and eccentric old figure standing quietly in his ancient coat seemed to embody all that was best in Partussian tradition. Here were the factors that made the Empire great: impartiality, bravery, disregard of self. The assembly burst into cheers.

Bowing slightly, fully solaced for the hell he had been through, Signatory Synvoret acknowledged their plaudits.

* * * *

So, for a brief while, the name Earth was a familiar one among the rulers of Partussy. Then, inevitably, interest in it drained away through sub-committee and under-council. There were, after all, four million planets to be dealt with. Eventually, the end result of the whole matter, a blue directive labelled "Restricted All Levels," and signed by Supremo Graylix of the Colony Worlds Council was stamped by a bored clerk in the Inferior Systems Office and sent to Earth by quickest means.

The day after this directive was received at Commission City, three men and a woman rode through a forest not many miles away.

The woman rode her horse with grace, resembling a portrait by Modigliani. She wore a blue blouse which matched the sapphire chips of her eyes. Her skin was brown, her hands slender on the rein. This, unmistakably, was Elizabeth Fallodon.

The man by her also sat easily on his horse, for he had picked a docile black mare. This discretion had turned riding, which he had once loathed, into one of his greatest pleasures. But there had been many changes in his way of living since Synvoret left, two years ago. These showed in his appearance. His deferential bearing had gone, the set of his shoulders was firmer. His expression, except when he turned to Elizabeth, had a certain fierceness in it, as if in his earlier years of self-questioning he had come at last on an unexpected answer. Now the pallor which years of living in a City had stamped upon him was gone. His face was as brown as an old sail. This man was Gary Towler.

Towler and Elizabeth, together with the two men who rode behind as escort, emerged from the forest into a curious landscape of dune and pampas, gully and bracken.

"A mile more and we shall be at Eastbon," Towler said. "We've come a roundabout way, but the quietest. Can you see the line of the escarpment ahead, between the dunes? There lies Eastbon. We are late. Peter Lardening will be there before us."

Looking at her with a smile he added, "It's two years and more since either of us saw him. You were fond of him once, Elizabeth, remember?"

"And so I still am. He saved your life."

Towler nodded to that and the implication behind it. He and his wife loved each other so strongly that there was room in their lives for a dozen other sorts of fondness. As they jogged along the winding track between tall grass, over ground that had once been sea bed, he fell to remembering those crowded events a couple of years ago in which Lardening had suddenly played an important part. The sun that burned on his shoulders became the smouldering heat of fear he had felt as he lay defenceless on the floor while the impregnable figure of Raggball bore down on him. . . .

Willing his limbs into action, Towler jumped up. As the Partussian bodyguard, slightly handicapped by his air suit, swung out an arm, Towler ducked under it. He dived for the knife. Raggball without hesitation threw the table at him, knocking him against the wall. Bounding forward, the great creature seized him by the arm.

A man appeared from the kitchen, gripping an old-fashioned terrestial explosive revolver in his hand. He fired twice.

The first shot shattered the glassite dome of Raggball's suit.

Suddenly on the defensive, the nul spun about. The second shot blasted one of his eye-stalks. Like a great battering ram, he charged with his full ton weight head first for the door, bursting through into the corridor.

Thrusting the gun into his pocket, Peter Lardening ran to Towler.

"Are you all right? Explanations later. We've got to get out of there before Chav has the place surrounded."

"I'm right behind you," Towler said shakily. He picked up his knife and they ran from the ruined room. Raggball was dying an oxygen death in the corridor. Already he was beyond interfering with them.

Lardening led the way down the street. They doubled along two side alleys and into a vegetable store. An ally of Lardening's was there. Nodding, he led them into a rear room. Without turning a hair, he sewed them in separate potato sacks and concealed them among similar sacks.

Outside, hooters sounded.

In no time, all of Arm Marshall Terekomy's available nuls were in the native quarter, with reinforcements continually coming up. The whole quarter was surrounded and searched. But the Marshall was overkeen. His police were so many they got in the way of each other. The store filled with them more than once, but the two interpreters were not discovered.

Par-Chavorlem himself arrived on the scene. Anxious to erase the violence which had been done to his honoured guest, he ordered the destruction of the entire native quarter. Demolition squads were formed, buildings were pulled down wholesale, while frightened refugees salvaged what belongings they could and fled from the area.

The result was chaos in the City. Unable to leave it, hundreds
118

of homeless people camped in the streets, piling their luggage and possessions about them. In the confusion, Lardening and Towler contacted the refuse man who had taken the latter to Rivars previously, and they rode out of the City on the midnight disposal cart.

"We're well out of that," Lardening exclaimed, as the two of them made their way on foot to Rivars' camp.

"We certainly stirred up a hornet's nest, but will the end result be for the better? If only I had killed Synvoret. . . ."

"Don't reproach yourself, Gary. You did well. Don't forget I overheard everything from the kitchen."

"I never saw you there."

Lardening chuckled.

"When you came in, I was squeezed behind the door. Besides you were preoccupied, to say the least."

"What were you doing there? I thought you were ill?"

"The illness was a fake to give you one more chance to speak to Synvoret, to give me a chance to search your place and retrieve the Starjjan foot. As you must have guessed by now, I too serve Rivars. He told you about me without mentioning my name. As the days went by and we saw you had still not given the evidence to Synvoret, we naturally mistrusted you." He paused with a certain embarrassment.

"Sometimes I mistrusted myself," Towler said sharply. "Go on."

"Rivars ordered me to kill you."

Again Towler had the choking sensation that assailed him when he thought of Rivars. More and more he came to look on the leader as an enemy. Here was proof that even the unimaginative Rivars felt that enmity too.

"By feigning illness and giving you another chance, I was disobeying Rivars," Lardening said. "He has no understanding of our difficulties in the City. As luck had it, I was raiding your rooms when you brought Synvoret in."

Though in the City it would be little more than one in the morning, out here the sky was pale ahead of them with a new dawn. By its growing light, Towler surveyed the other.

"Your help was more than welcome. You must know how grateful I am. If only you had declared yourself to me some days ago, you could have helped me even more."

"I know that. But then Rivars had not informed me you were also his agent. We could have worked in co-operation

119

had he not been so secretive. However, whether we have succeeded or failed, at least we've done."

"Yes," said Towler. "For good or ill our work in the City's finished. We can be of little further use to Rivars now."

They walked on in silence. Twice Partussian ships roared overhead, and they hid themselves in bushes rather than risk discovery.

They had been travelling for less than half an hour when noises ahead brought them to a halt. Once again they concealed themselves. Listening carefully, they could make out that a considerable party of humans was coming in their direction. The party was keeping quiet and advancing with some haste. After a minute, heads were visible above the tangle of foliage to their front.

Towler stood up and said in a loud voice, "Friends are here."

He was surprised to find a column of men, most of them well-armed but battle weary, ahead of him. From the leaders of the column Towler and Lardening learnt that they represented the survivors of a larger body of Rivars' men which had been cut off by the Starjjans. Now they were retreating from a nul patrol.

"What's been happening in the City?" the column leader asked. "Is there a crisis on? Recently the nuls have been happy just to contain us. Now they're picking us off as fast as they can."

"Someone tried to bump off Chav's visiting signatory," Towler said. "As a result, he's turned nasty and is pulling the place to pieces. But you people are only heading into trouble. You've lost your bearings; another half hour's march will bring you to the City itself."

"We've got the nuls behind us. We'll have to continue," the column leader replied, but he stood there indecisively. Towler's eyes ran over his troop. Several women were among them. One was stepping out of line now and coming towards him, a tall and willowy figure. It was Elizabeth.

Next minute they were pressed together, their arms round each other.

Half laughing, half weeping, she said, "I wanted to help you so much, Gary, my dearest! Yet I've never reached Rivars at all. I thought that if I could get out of the City and meet him, I could make him understand how awkward your position was."

120

"Rivars' precious chunk of evidence arrived just after you left," Towler said, holding both her hands. "But why didn't you leave me a note to say what you were doing?. You don't know how I felt when you just disappeared."

"I did leave a note."

"I never found it!"

Lardening came forward, looking from one to the other of them guiltily.

"I'm sorry about this, Elizabeth," he said, "but I found that note and destroyed it. Do you remember you asked me to meet you in a café? And I walked out rather foolishly. Almost at once I regretted the way I had behaved. I went around to your flat to apologize, and found the note lying there. Anyone might have found it, and then you'd all have been incriminated, so I destroyed it."

Elizabeth regarded him curiously, a slight smile on her lips.

"But I worded my note so that only Gary would understand it."

Lardening looked quickly at her, then away, gnawing his lips and murmuring that he had thought the note was better destroyed. When Gary looked as if he were about to pursue the subject, Elizabeth laid a restraining hand on his arm. She had gathered that Lardening's reason for destroying the note was less caution than jealousy.

"It doesn't matter in any case," she said. "Although I managed to get out of the City, I never managed to reach Rivars. From this side, the Varne Heights are crawling with Starjjans. I met up with this isolated party and have been with them ever since. We don't even seem to know where we're heading."

Towler and Lardening explained the situation as they saw it. Wearily, the rest of the party sprawled in the grass, eating rations or lighting up aphrohales, too tired to be other than indifferent to the discussion going on at their head.

"So we're near the disposal dump, where we can get on to the main road," Elizabeth was saying reflectively. "What time would it be in the City now, Peter?"

Lardening calculated.

"About two in the morning," he said.

"Three hours till their dawn. Time enough. ... Listen, I've got a plan. It sounds crazy and perhaps you'll say it couldn't work, but ... would you like to hear it?"

They sat and listened to Elizabeth's plan in wondering silence. It had many of the elements of the mind that produced it. It was not complex, yet it had wit and some recklessness, and it managed to be, though obvious, unexpected.

"By God, we'll do it if we all get killed in the attempt!" Towler cried, jumping up. "Elizabeth, my dear, you're a genius! Elizabeth, if this comes off we're – we're unbeatable!"

In a little more than an hour the party had marched back to the disposal plant and taken up defensive positions there. The plant was purely automatic, so that they were not disturbed as they piled cans of unconsumed rubbish across the great road. Their maximum fire power was then concentrated at two points, one group being concealed behind the wall of the plant where they could cover the road, the other actually in the road where the piled cans hid them from the view of anyone approaching from the City.

They ran a certain risk in being discovered by vehicles moving towards the City, but at this time of day traffic was always negligible.

Then came the wait. They crouched in their positions until the twenty-six hour schedule of the City brought another artificial dawn there. Time crept by.

"They will be along any minute now," Towler said in a low voice at last. He lay behind the low plant wall nursing a gun, Elizabeth and Lardening beside him with other members of the party. The column leader commanded the party behind the roadblock.

Five minutes later a meuron defence truck and three other nul vehicles appeared from the direction of the City, moving fast, a foot above the ground. This was the daily dawn convoy taking orders and supplies to Par-Chavorlem's concealed City.

The vehicles nosed up to the block and stopped, sinking lightly to rest on the surface of the road as their compression died. Three nuls jumped down out of each truck, hurrying forward to investigate.

The ambush parties opened fire.

Even a virtually unkillable Partussian cannot survive when his body is nearly blown to bits. When the barrage of fire vanished, twelve bodies, bulky and heavy as whales, lay lifeless in the road. Cheering, the terrestials surged forward.

The corpses were dragged away, the barrier of cans removed. Everyone worked as if inspired. The trucks were seized, their contents flung into the road. Armed men climbed aboard.

"Gary, a lot of us will have to stay here. I want to stay," Lardening said, taking Towler's sleeve as the ex-interpreter swung himself up into one of the cabs.

"No, Peter, you must come. We can't leave you here to be mopped up," Towler said. "Jump aboard."

"I won't be mopped up. There's a useful job I can do. I'll make it to Rivars on my own to tell him what is happening, what you're doing. Then we will join you as soon as possible."

"You must come with us, Peter," Elizabeth said. "We'll get a message through to Rivars later."

He looked her straight in the eyes.

"You go on with Gary, Elizabeth," he said. "I think for a while I'll be better on my own."

Armed now with the infinitely superior nul weapons, the new owners of the trucks moved off under Towler's command. The column leader was to follow up on foot with the remainder of the party. They gave a rousing cheer as the trucks surged forward, rising slightly above the vulcanized road as they gathered speed.

So the big City fell to Earth.

Unsuspecting nul guards let the convoy in through the main gates as usual before falling beneath its withering fire. In a few hours the whole skeleton staff of nuls in the City had been wiped out. It involved surprisingly little in the way of actual fighting, Towler simply seizing the Atmosphere Plant and pumping oxygen in everywhere.

The City was impregnable, beyond retribution.

The column leader's party arrived at the gates later that day. News of Earth's great victory spread fast. In troops or singly, Earthmen filtered in to what had been a prison and was now a bastion.

Sure in his own power, Towler at once sent out offers of peace to the Starjjan leaders. Within three days an armistice had been signed. Starjjans too filtered into the big City. In little time it was garrisoned by a considerable fighting force.

The entire manoeuvre took Par-Chavorlem and Terekomy completely by surprise. But it was something other than shock that delayed their retaliation. They could not move effectively until Synvoret left. The big City was illegal, a gigantic material witness to their misrule. Whatever happened – and the very

123

worst had happened – they could not risk letting the Signatory suspect its existence.

Twenty minutes after the *Geboraa* had blasted for Partussy with Synvoret and his party aboard, Par-Chavorlem's forces struck and were repulsed. The big City was impregnable, as Par-Chavorlem had intended it to be.

"You're a miracle-worker," Elizabeth told Towler admiringly.

"So are you, my dearest. I told you we both had tigers in us."

All these thoughts and memories passed through Gary Towler's mind as he jogged on his mare towards Eastbon with his wife Elizabeth beside him.

He was a leader now, and Rivars was dead. Rivars had refused to come to the City. Rivars feared the Cities, and knew only his outlaw life in the wilds. When most of his men had deserted him for Towler, he roved the Channel Valley with a small guerilla band until the nul patrols shot him down. Peter Lardening, with him at the time, escaped. Lardening then remained in the area to keep open the tenuous and hazardous link with the spies inside Par-Chavorlem's City. It was Lardening who had gathered the news Towler now came personally to receive.

Into the centre of the town they rode. Men and women ran out to greet them, waving and calling. Human beings now lived more comfortably than before in the old towns. Though Par-Chavorlem's punitive expeditions were as recklessly frequent as ever, terrestials were armed now with the stereosonic weapons stored in the big City. Their strength equalled Par-Chavorlem's. Their numbers grew larger daily.

Towler and Elizabeth rode into a fortified area in the middle of the town. An officer came up, saluted, and asked them to dismount. Willing hands took their horses to water them.

"Please come with me, sir," the officer said.

They followed him into a ruined arcade, their footsteps echoing against the derelict shops. From the far end came Peter Lardening, hurrying to meet them.

"Well met, Gary! Well met, Elizabeth! You look as lovely as ever, if Gary will allow me to say so. We meet after two years, and I have the best of news to greet you with."

They shook each other's hands, smiling and laughing. It was easier to smile than it had been during the last thousand years. Hope was alive again. Men were awake again. Soldiery was on the march, aspiration on the wing.

Greetings over, Lardening led them into one of the shattered shops which had been turned into a temporary office. They drank wine and toasted each other.

"Come on then, Peter," Elizabeth said. "What's the great news you have for us? What verdict did Partussy pass on Synvoret's report? I hope your spies have brought you a full statement?"

Lardening smiled at them both, enjoying keeping them in suspense. He leaned against the wall, thrusting his hands into his pockets with an air of assumed nonchalance.

"The Supremo of the Colony Worlds Council has dismissed Par-Chavorlem and his retinue from office. . . ."

For a moment they let him get no further, shouting their exultation. When he finished the rest of what he had to say, they burst into incredulous laughter.

"It can't be!" Towler exclaimed. "Who knows of all this but you, Peter?"

"Nobody, of course. I saved it for you. It's far too good to squander!"

"Indeed it is. But we must share it, share it with everybody. Come on, Elizabeth! Let's tell the crowd outside. This is the richest joke for thirty generations."

With the others behind him, he ran down the broken arcade out into the sunshine.

His eyes gleaming, he climbed up on to a cart. When people saw who he was they came running even before he called to them. They flocked about the cart, a crowd who already scented excitement.

He looked down at them, a shaggy-headed lot who were destined to form virtually a new race. He looked around at the crumbling buildings, the dead shell of an old world, the wombing place of a new. He looked up at the sky, where the rulers of the galaxy were too far distant and no longer powerful enough to intervene in Earth's affairs. Then he looked down again at the faces raised to his.

"Friends, I have great news, the only news worth hearing! Par-Chavorlem, our hated enemy and exploiter, is going. His bosses have booted him out before we managed it! He and all his retinue have their orders to leave for Castacorze and thence to Partussy within the week."

The cheers came up and took him by the throat. He smiled at Elizabeth, so poised and complete, at Peter Lardening, so eager and courageous.

"Hear the rest of it and the best of it," he called, as the hubbub died down. "A new Commissioner is already on his way here. He is not a nul but a Dlotpodite, a species bound to look sympathetically on our struggle and to reach agreement with us."

The crowd interrupted him again, but he stilled them.

"We shall avoid bloodshed if possible. There's been too much of it on Earth. Fortunately, with the big City in our hands, we are in a position of power, and I do not doubt that we shall secure complete independence and the banishment of every single Partussian from Earth. Then we shall see to it that Earth becomes like a guiding light to other subject worlds!"

Again the crowd began to interrupt, but he silenced them with a raised hand. Command came easily to him now.

"You may ask how it is that Par-Chavorlem has been recalled, when all our efforts to communicate the truth about him to Synvoret failed. The answer is that when Synvoret reported my attempt on his life to his superiors, they were very poorly impressed. Our spies in the enemy HQ have sent us the text of the message that dismisses Par-Chavorlem. So we know the reason why he has got the sack. We know that he is going because Partussy judges him to be altogether too lax to rule us."

"Par-Chavorlem too lax. . . . Too lax. . . ." His words were repeated through the crowd with growing amusement.

Towler watched them. Then his face relaxed and he began to laugh, partly from the irony of it, partly from sheer light-heartedness. There was no word for how he felt, either in his own tongue or in Partussian.

The crowd was infected with his mirth. More people were pouring in, smiling even before they heard what the joke was. Elizabeth and Lardening were chuckling again. The laughter spread like floodwater, catching up men in other streets who knew not why they laughed. Even the soldiers at the barricades found their set features relaxing and their guard momentarily down. It was as if a great purgative merriment had seized the whole ancient town before sweeping out until its last ripples reached the last corners of the globe.

In the bright sunlight, it was as if everyone was suddenly laughing.

126

NEL BESTSELLERS

Crime

T013 332	CLOUDS OF WITNESS	*Dorothy L. Sayers*	40p
T016 307	THE UNPLEASANTNESS AT THE BELLONA CLUB	*Dorothy L. Sayers*	40p
T021 548	GAUDY NIGHT	*Dorothy L. Sayers*	40p
T026 698	THE NINE TAILORS	*Dorothy L. Sayers*	50p
T026 671	FIVE RED HERRINGS	*Dorothy L. Sayers*	50p
T015 556	MURDER MUST ADVERTISE	*Dorothy L. Sayers*	40p

Fiction

T018 520	HATTER'S CASTLE	*A. J. Cronin*	75p
T013 944	CRUSADER'S TOMB	*A. J. Cronin*	60p
T013 936	THE JUDAS TREE	*A. J. Cronin*	50p
T015 386	THE NORTHERN LIGHT	*A. J. Cronin*	50p
T026 213	THE CITADEL	*A. J. Cronin*	80p
T027 112	BEYOND THIS PLACE	*A. J. Cronin*	60p
T016 609	KEYS OF THE KINGDOM	*A. J. Cronin*	50p
T027 201	THE STARS LOOK DOWN	*A. J. Cronin*	90p
T018 539	A SONG OF SIXPENCE	*A. J. Cronin*	50p
T001 288	THE TROUBLE WITH LAZY ETHEL	*Ernest K. Gann*	30p
T003 922	IN THE COMPANY OF EAGLES	*Ernest K. Gann*	30p
T023 001	WILDERNESS BOY	*Stephen Harper*	35p
T017 524	MAGGIE D	*Adam Kennedy*	60p
T022 390	A HERO OF OUR TIME	*Mikhail Lermontov*	45p
T025 691	SIR, YOU BASTARD	*G. F. Newman*	40p
T022 536	THE HARRAD EXPERIMENT	*Robert H. Rimmer*	50p
T022 994	THE DREAM MERCHANTS	*Harold Robbins*	95p
T023 303	THE PIRATE	*Harold Robbins*	95p
T022 968	THE CARPETBAGGERS	*Harold Robbins*	£1·00
T016 560	WHERE LOVE HAS GONE	*Harold Robbins*	75p
T023 958	THE ADVENTURERS	*Harold Robbins*	£1·00
T025 241	THE INHERITORS	*Harold Robbins*	90p
T025 276	STILETTO	*Harold Robbins*	50p
T025 268	NEVER LEAVE ME	*Harold Robbins*	50p
T025 292	NEVER LOVE A STRANGER	*Harold Robbins*	90p
T022 226	A STONE FOR DANNY FISHER	*Harold Robbins*	80p
T025 284	79 PARK AVENUE	*Harold Robbins*	75p
T025 187	THE BETSY	*Harold Robbins*	80p
T020 894	RICH MAN, POOR MAN	*Irwin Shaw*	90p

Historical

T022 196	KNIGHT WITH ARMOUR	*Alfred Duggan*	50p
T022 250	THE LADY FOR RANSOM	*Alfred Duggan*	50p
T015 297	COUNT BOHEMOND	*Alfred Duggan*	50p
T017 958	FOUNDING FATHERS	*Alfred Duggan*	50p
T017 753	WINTER QUARTERS	*Alfred Duggan*	50p
T021 297	FAMILY FAVOURITES	*Alfred Duggan*	50p
T022 625	LEOPARDS AND LILIES	*Alfred Duggan*	60p
T019 624	THE LITTLE EMPERORS	*Alfred Duggan*	50p
T020 126	THREE'S COMPANY	*Alfred Duggan*	50p
T021 300	FOX 10: BOARDERS AWAY	*Adam Hardy*	35p

Science Fiction

T016 900	STRANGER IN A STRANGE LAND	*Robert Heinlein*	75p
T020 797	STAR BEAST	*Robert Heinlein*	35p
T017 451	I WILL FEAR NO EVIL	*Robert Heinlein*	80p
T026 817	THE HEAVEN MAKERS	*Frank Herbert*	35p
T027 279	DUNE	*Frank Herbert*	90p
T022 854	DUNE MESSIAH	*Frank Herbert*	60p
T023 974	THE GREEN BRAIN	*Frank Herbert*	35p
T012 859	QUEST FOR THE FUTURE	*A. E. Van Vogt*	35p
T015 270	THE WEAPON MAKERS	*A. E. Van Vogt*	30p
T023 265	EMPIRE OF THE ATOM	*A. E. Van Vogt*	40p
T017 354	THE FAR-OUT WORLDS OF A. E. VAN VOGT	*A. E. Van Vogt*	40p

....

NEL P.O. BOX 11, FALMOUTH, CORNWALL

For U.K. & Eire: customers should include to cover postage, 15p for the first book plus 5p per copy for each additional book ordered, up to a maximum charge of 50p.

For Overseas customers & B.F.P.O.: customers should include to cover postage, 20p for the first book and 10p per copy for each additional book.

Name ....

Address...

....

Title ....
(MAY)